# THING WE LOST

*Loving Locksley: Book 1*

**SHAE BANKS**

# CONTENTS

| | |
|---|---:|
| Chapter 1 | 1 |
| Chapter 2 | 6 |
| Chapter 3 | 12 |
| Chapter 4 | 20 |
| Chapter 5 | 28 |
| Chapter 6 | 34 |
| Chapter 7 | 40 |
| Chapter 8 | 50 |
| Chapter 9 | 57 |
| Chapter 10 | 63 |
| Chapter 11 | 70 |
| Chapter 12 | 78 |
| Chapter 13 | 86 |
| Chapter 14 | 93 |
| Chapter 15 | 99 |
| Chapter 16 | 109 |
| Chapter 17 | 116 |
| Chapter 18 | 124 |
| Chapter 19 | 133 |
| Chapter 20 | 138 |
| Chapter 21 | 145 |
| Chapter 22 | 152 |
| Chapter 23 | 158 |
| About the Author | 169 |

Mistakes are always forgivable, if one has the courage to admit them.
Bruce Lee

Copyright © 2019 by Shae Banks
All rights reserved. This book or any portion thereof
may not be reproduced or used in any manner whatsoever
without the express written permission of the publisher
except for the use of brief quotations in a book review.
Cover by LKO design
Editing by Hourglass Editing
and
Elemental Editing and Proofreading
Formatting by Kassie Morse
For more on the author please visit:
www.shaebanks.com

# CHAPTER ONE

Interviews always made me nervous. I hated being under the microscope, answering questions, and trying to make myself sound interesting. I was qualified. I needed to get out of my current position. I wasn't happy, and if I'd learned one thing in my thirty years, it's that life is too short to be miserable.

I'd have more free time. I wasn't sure what I was going to do with it, probably more exercise, but like my best friend Haylie said, it was better than sitting in traffic for two hours every night.

Locking the car, I walked toward the building as I straightened my jacket and fiddled with the strap of my bag.

The steel structure gleamed in the morning sunlight and the blackout windows to the right gave nothing away. To the left was what looked to be a workshop with several large white trucks all lined up outside and LGW Solutions written on the sides in royal blue.

The same logo was printed on the front door. I took a deep breath before stepping inside and stopped short as the girl at the reception desk looked at me with a bored expression. She was around twenty, and her hair was sculpted into a perfect, glossy bun on top of her head. Her eyes narrowed, her impeccably groomed brows not moving at all, while her perfectly drawn eyeliner accentuated the expression of judgement and distaste. Snotty bitch.

"Hi, I'm Nathalie Johnson. I'm here to see… Cara?"

"Fill this out, and take a seat over there."

She handed me a form, and I scanned it. "Umm… I have one of…" She gave me another frosty look, and I mumbled, "Never mind."

Sitting on one of the brand-new chairs opposite her desk, I opened my bag and withdrew the completed form identical to the one she'd handed me. Clearly over prepared. I wasn't sure if that was a bad sign, but I was so sick of working in payroll. This job was better suited for me. A smaller office. A quieter work environment. Okay, so eyebrows at the desk made me feel about as welcome as a dose of the clap, but I didn't have to like her, I just had to work with her. *If* I got the job.

"Nathalie?"

The accent was southern. London, maybe? I turned my head and smiled.

The woman in front of me was much taller than me. A pretty blonde, with tanned skin and perfect makeup. Her tiny waist was accentuated by the tight fit of her bodycon dress, and I could tell with a glance her heels were Louboutin's. I smiled at her and stood. "Yeah. Yes."

I don't know why I was so nervous. I'd had dozens of interviews. None in the last three years, admittedly, but she made me… self-conscious. Okay, so my inferiority complex was deeply ingrained, but I knew I had what she needed. I could get through the interview regardless of her perfect appearance and her beautiful shoes, and prove it.

"Don't be nervous. We're a family company, we pride ourselves on being approachable," she said smiling. "We're in here."

I followed, still clutching the form, and stepped into the office, looking around. My attention was immediately drawn to the guy sitting at the desk, mobile to his ear, a broad grin on his face. "Yeah, yeah definitely. Just stick her around the back and take off, Rich needs that kit down at the site. Yeah, mate, you too. Got to go. See you Friday." He ended the call and turned the mobile to silent before looking at me, getting to his feet, and stepping around the desk. He was tall, athletic, and dark haired, with a neat beard and sharply dressed in a suit. Holding out a hand, he said, "Nathalie. Thanks for coming in, it's a pleasure to meet you. I'm Tony, and you've met Cara."

I did my best to smile, then looked down at his extended hand. I forced myself to take it, shook it, then looked back at Cara. She gave me an encouraging nod and gestured to the chair opposite him. Strangely, she took the seat beside me.

"Your resume made for an interesting read, Nathalie. You're overqualified for the role as I'm sure you know. Can I start by asking why you applied for the position? Business Administrator is something of a step down from Senior Finance Administrator."

Shit. Shit, shit, shit. I did have an answer prepared, but my head emptied. He was looking at me with his head cocked to one side, waiting for an answer, and I could feel my heart starting to beat a little faster under his scrutiny. "Umm... honestly? I need something... easier. Not that I think this would be easy, it wouldn't. I don't mean... It's just that's such a massive company and the workload never changes. Ever. There's no challenge in it. There's no community. Add to that the hell of a commute," I looked up at the ceiling and took a breath, "this place is walking distance from my house. If the weather's nice, I can walk into work. If the weather is awful, I can still get into work. No sitting in traffic for two hours..." I was rambling and decided it's best I shut up.

I watched him, waiting for a reaction, and when his brows twitched, a small line forming between them, I knew I'd completely messed it up. Damn nerves had killed my chance of getting out of that god-awful place I'd been slowly dying in, professionally speaking.

"We noticed a two-year gap in your employment history, Nathalie," Cara said. My heart sank further. "The only explanation you gave was illness."

This question I was prepared for. "Yes. It was a period of rehabilitation following a road traffic accident. It took a while to recover, there was a significant amount of physical therapy as well as several surgeries, but I used that time to gain my Finance and Management degree. I have made a full recovery and my health has improved every year since," I said. It was the only well-practiced line I had. It was the only thing anyone ever wanted to talk about after I let them know about it. It was never going away, but the subject wasn't in my top ten thousand talking points. It was easier to give the practiced response and hope they moved on quickly.

Cara smiled. It wasn't the usual apologetic one, and she didn't scan me for obvious clues as to what had been damaged, which was nice. "I'm glad to hear it. Any commitments we would need to know about? Physical therapy appointments for example, so accommodations can be made for your absence."

My only thought was, *wow*. Most places would run a damn mile. Did that mean I had the job? "Oh, no. Thank you. I'm fine. I have a relatively intense workout schedule that keeps me in half decent shape. I don't rely on meds for pain relief or anything like that, I've been lucky. The odd ache or pain during the winter, but that doesn't affect my day-to-day activities."

She smiled, made a note, then looked at Tony.

"Do you have any family, Nathalie?" he asked.

I shook my head. "No. I'm divorced. No children, no partner, no parents, no siblings. Mum was the last to go, died of cancer a couple of years ago."

He nodded once, his lips pressed into a grim line, then he smiled and said, "Well, Nathalie. There were twenty applicants, but the rest didn't touch your credentials. What is your required period of notice with your current employer?"

I frowned. Confused. "Umm, two weeks, but I'm currently off for two weeks, so if I emailed them today, I think, technically, I'm free from tomorrow."

He smiled, physically relaxing. "Well, no need to rob you of two weeks off. Take your holiday, work the notice period to prevent any complications, and we'll see you here at nine AM on Tuesday the twenty-third."

I looked from him to Cara. "Really? That's it?"

She gave me a warm smile and replied, "That's it. We'll have everything ready for you. Enjoy your time off."

And that was my dismissal, apparently, as the two of them got to their feet. Tony shook my hand again, and Cara escorted me out.

After thanks and goodbyes, I walked out of there wondering how the hell that had happened. This was my worst interview ever. I don't know why I panicked. Maybe it was Tony and his lovely smile. Maybe it was Cara and her relaxed and friendly approach. Whatever, it seemed to do the job.

I sent a text to Haylie, my best and only friend, before starting my car. I had two weeks off and was finally free of that shitty payroll department. Friday night, I was celebrating.

## CHAPTER TWO

Haylie's cackle rang out over the speakers above our heads. "You're a lucky bitch, Nat."

I didn't usually feel lucky, no one had worse luck than me. Every time things looked up, shit happened. But, just this once, she had a point. I raised my glass, and she chinked hers against it.

"Seriously, though. I'm so happy for you. No more Moody Mandy!"

Mandy was my manager and she was a bitch. Mandy could stick her job right up her arse.

I grinned at my friend and drained my glass. "Need to pee. No, don't get up, I won't be long."

We'd gone through two bottles of wine in an hour, and I wasn't feeling particularly steady. Regardless, we were meeting some of her work friends in a club later, and there were several hours left of my celebratory night out.

I was walking up the stairs to the bathrooms when I tripped. I'm good at that, falling upstairs. Especially after so much wine. I hastily looked around to see if anyone had seen it and was relieved when I found myself alone on the staircase. I snorted to myself, turned the corner, and walked straight into a large, solid body.

"I'm sorry, love. Are you all right?"

Swallowing hard, my stomach clenched, and I froze. I knew that voice. The accent was off, but the voice was one I'd heard a million times. You don't forget your ex-boyfriend's voice. I panicked. "I'm sorry, I wasn't looking, yeah, I'm fine. Sorry." I was spluttering, keeping my head down and trying to sidestep him without making eye contact, but his hand settled on my upper arm.

I looked up, and the air left my lungs.

I hadn't seen that face in thirteen years. It was the same face. Older. I hated to admit it, but handsomer. His eyes were just as blue. His hair was longer. Skin was darker. The few days growth along his jaw gave him a slightly rugged look that suited him. The tight t-shirt he wore suggested he looked after himself and spent more than a few hours in the gym. I didn't focus on any one part of him for long, looking back up at his face.

His lips twitched in a nervous smile. "Nat?"

His voice was exactly as I remembered it. It still had the same effect on me. "Jason?"

His eyes were all over my face, flicking here and there, scanning my features, noting the changes. "God... How are you?"

He'd dropped his accent, but I suppose that's what people did when they moved away. He must have gotten in with a bunch of southerners and been forced to drop it.

*He ran away*, a small voice in the back of my mind reminded me. He ran away, and dumped me to go to university.

We started dating when we were fifteen. He was my first boyfriend. My first kiss. My first sexual partner. He'd been my everything. My soulmate. We were supposed to stay that way forever, but he brought that to an abrupt end.

I never knew why he left. I never knew what I'd done wrong.

I didn't want to know now.

"I'm... I... Excuse me..."

I pushed past him and into the bathroom. After four very large glasses of wine, and climbing two flights of stairs, I was desperate. And I didn't know what I was supposed to say to him.

In the safety of the lady's bathroom, I locked the cubicle door and practically collapsed onto the toilet. I couldn't believe it, of all the people to bump into it had to be him.

I took my time, washing my hands and reapplying lipstick, before going back out. I knew he'd wait. I knew he'd be standing against the wall, watching the door, waiting for me to come back out. He'd want to talk to me, ask me questions, catch up. I didn't know what I was supposed to say.

His smile sent a zing of excitement through me. It always had. It was exactly how I remembered it, the dimples in his cheeks and twinkle in his eyes. I tucked my hair behind my ear and smiled nervously as I walked toward him.

"Nat, you look…" He bent to kiss my cheek. It was an innocent enough gesture when we hadn't seen each other in so long, but I stepped back, wrapping my arms around myself. I tried not to shrink away, but I didn't manage it.

I did manage to force the smile to stay put and mumble, "Hiya. How have you been?"

He looked uncomfortable and shoved his hands in his jeans pockets. "Good. Can I get you a drink? Catch up?"

Chewing my thumbnail, I pretended to consider. There was no way I could sit and have a drink with him. Not after everything. Not after all those years, although an explanation would be nice. "I'm with a friend. I should go, she'll wonder what's taking me so long. Nice seeing you, Jase."

He watched me pass, not bothering to ask again and even stepped out of my way. I glanced up at him as I walked by and saw the disappointment in his eyes.

*Good*, I told myself as I hurried down the stairs. I'd felt it for long enough.

I was aware of his gaze all the way to the bottom of the stairs. But there was no sound of footsteps, so I was sure he hadn't followed me down. I wasn't certain if that was because he picked up on my unease or because I had offended him. I didn't really care, I was just grateful he hadn't been on my heels.

Back in the bar, I relaxed a little and returned to our table.

"I was about to come looking," Haylie said as I slid back into my seat and necked my drink. "Shit, what's up with you?"

I poured another glass from bottle and drank half of that too. "I just bumped into Jason."

Her eyebrows lifted. "Locksley?"

I nodded, sucking on an ice cube that had slipped into my mouth as I drank. "Yep. He was on the landing."

"Shit... Is he still fit?" she asked. I looked away, and she burst out laughing. "What did you say to him?"

"Nothing," I said a little too quickly, feeling my cheeks heat. I took a mouthful of wine, catching another ice cube in my mouth. "He asked me if I wanted a drink, I said no, and I came back here."

"Shame. Could have scratched that itch."

"What itch?"

She flashed her brows at me just as Jason came through the doors that led to the toilets and walked toward us. I choked on my ice cube and looked down at the table, hoping he wouldn't see me.

He saw me.

"What's wrong?" she asked, then looked over her shoulder. "All right, Jase?"

I wanted the ground to open up and swallow me. Unfortunately, the bar stayed as it was, and he stopped at our table. "Hello Haylie. How've you been?"

She grinned up at him, ignoring me entirely. "I'm good. We're celebrating. Nat got a new job. Want to join us?"

He looked at me and smiled. I hoped he'd turn and face her, but he didn't. He looked directly into my eyes as he said, "Congratulations. Sorry, I can't, I'm out with a friend. Maybe next time. Have a good night."

I tried to smile and grabbed my drink, suddenly finding the remaining ice cubes incredibly interesting. I didn't say anything, and after a few seconds he walked away.

"Fucking hell," she said when he was gone. "He's improved with age. Did you see a wedding ring? I didn't. Do you think he's single?"

I poked at the ice cubes with my finger. "I honestly don't give a shit, Hayles."

She gave me that look. The one that meant 'don't give me that crap.'

"You can't still be pissed at him?"

I looked at her stony faced. "Not pissed, no," I said, although that wasn't entirely true. I'd never really forgiven him. I didn't think I ever would. The whole 'we were just kids' argument didn't stop me from feeling resentful. Seeing him brought it all fizzing and bubbling to the surface after years of being buried. But there was the other feeling, too. I ignored that one. "But I'm not exactly thrilled to see him."

She shook her head and sniffed at me.

I stuck out my tongue. "I'll go grab us another round."

I got up and grabbed my clutch, turning toward the bar. It wasn't too busy since it was still early, and I scanned the room to make sure he wasn't nearby. I couldn't see him, so I assumed he'd left with whoever he was with and breathed a sigh of relief.

I was served straight away which was odd. Three other guys were standing at the bar before I made it there. Not one to queue unnecessarily, I said, "Bottle of wine, please."

He plonked it on the bar in front of me. "Nat, yeah?"

"Yeah…"

"Jase said to have a good night."

I clenched my teeth but didn't say anything. I just grabbed the bottle and returned to our table.

"That was quick," Haylie said, taking the jug from me.

"It was all ready for me," I explained, sliding down the bench opposite her. "Jase left it. Said to have a good night."

She gave me a toothy grin and poured herself a glass. "How much are you betting he turns up later?"

I scowled. "He better bloody not. If he does, he'll be told where to go."

She wagged a finger at me, grinning broadly. "This is a sign, Nat. I'm telling you."

I shook my head and refreshed my glass. "I thought we were here to celebrate my new job?"

She rolled her eyes then raised her glass. "To fresh starts."

I chinked my glass against hers and took a sip. "Yeah. Fresh starts." It wasn't until she snorted into her glass that I realized what I'd just toasted to. Bitch.

## CHAPTER THREE

My first week at work went as I expected. The receptionist I'd met before the interview, Chantal, was slightly less frosty but not exactly welcoming. I had the feeling she was going to be a thorn in my side. By the end of the week, I wondered if her expression was due to too much Botox, because her forehead and cheeks didn't seem to move during any situation. Her face was just fixed in the same dour expression all the time.

Cara was there for my first morning, and she was great at showing me the ropes. The other people in the office seemed okay but were quiet. Sandra, the Admin Manager, appeared to be in charge the second Cara wasn't around, and she gave me piles of invoices I was to work through each morning before assigning me other things to do.

Friday afternoon, Tony came out and told us all to go home half an hour early. Tony, it turned out, was probably the best boss I'd ever had. If he needed anything, he always said 'please' and if I delivered something, he always said 'thank you.' It was a refreshing change from the shitty attitudes I faced in my last job.

"You're ready for a couple of days off, aren't you?" he asked as I shut down my computer.

I gave a small laugh. "I've had a great week, actually."

It was true, I had really enjoyed going to work. He looked around the room with his hands in his pockets. The silence was awkward, so I asked, "Have you got anything planned?"

"The usual. A few beers with friends, watch a match." I think he was going to ask what I was doing when his phone rang.

"Yeah? Okay. Yeah, I'll wait here and give you a lift. Okay, mate." Tucking the phone into his trousers pocket, he smiled. "That's me stuck here another hour. Have a good weekend, Nathalie."

I smiled, tucked my hair behind my ear, and moved to the door. "You too. See you Monday."

I sat in my car, watching the cleaner arrive, and sent Haylie a message asking if she fancied a few drinks in town. Her response was immediate and affirmative, as I'd known it would be, so I set off for home to get ready.

* * *

By six forty-five I was in our favorite bar with a bottle of wine on ice, waiting for Haylie. I'd poured myself a glass and tried to relax as I looked around the room. Three tables down were a group of young girls. I pushed the self-conscious feeling away and picked up my phone, keeping myself busy browsing through my social media accounts. I hadn't been on for a couple of days, busy with work, and was surprised to see a friend request waiting for me. I opened it up and groaned when I saw Jason's name. Chewing my lip, I let my thumb hover over the accept icon for a second but changed my mind at the last moment and closed the app.

I was still looking at the blank screen when Haylie turned up.

"God, it's pissing down. If that doesn't stop, I'm spending all night in here."

I smiled at her and put my phone away. "It was fine when I got here. How's your week been?"

Haylie worked with adults with learning disabilities, a high-pressure job by all accounts, and not something I could have ever done, but she was brilliant. It was a calling, and she loved every minute of it. She couldn't tell me the ins and outs due to confidentiality, but she usually had a little something to share.

She fluffed her damp hair and sat down, pouring herself a glass of wine. "Shit."

I shook my head. "Is that it or...?"

"Fucking Paul moved me to the late shift next week. I don't work fucking late shifts, I work earlies. I get in, I get it done, I get the fuck out."

"And what did he say when you told him that?" I knew she had, in those exact words. She was an absolute diamond, but she was a rough one, and she wasn't one to mince her words.

She gulped down a mouthful of her drink. "Well, he said either I worked what he put me down for, or I didn't work at all. Jumped up prick. I don't know why Julie gave him the off duty, he's a little fucking Hitler with it."

"So, what are you doing about it?"

She gulped another mouthful of wine. "Work the bastard late shift."

I pressed my lips together, trying not to laugh.

"What about you? How was the first week?"

"It was surprisingly good," I said enthusiastically. "They're all a bit quiet, but the boss is nice. He let us go early today, and he won't dock my pay for it, and the other boss who isn't always in was around Monday. Yeah, think I'm going to like it."

"You're a lucky bitch," she groused, shaking her head and laughing.

"Oi, I keep telling you, I had my share of bad luck, Hayles. I think it's my turn."

She raised her glass and tilted her head to the side. "Yes, it is. Speaking of luck. Seen anything else of Jase?"

She raised her brows at me as she refilled our glasses. I breathed in heavily and replied, "Nope. It's been a month. I have a friend request.

I didn't accept it. He hasn't made another attempt to contact me, so I'm assuming he's taken the hint."

"I can't believe you told him to jog on."

I shrugged. "I can't open that one back up. I've come too far to go right back to where it bloody started. I'm better off on my own."

She tried not to give me a sad look, but I saw the brief flicker in her eyes. She was wrong, I didn't need anyone. I was safer on my own.

"Anyway, I don't need a bloke to be happy any more than you do," I told her indignantly.

She sniggered at that. "Speak for yourself. I get mine."

I didn't want to get into her sex life. That wasn't for me. Her relationship with her boyfriend was far too turbulent for my liking. I needed something a bit more stable and I wasn't going to get that chasing Jason Locksley. He'd already proven how unreliable he was. I honestly would rather be alone. I looked at her with a brow cocked. "Oh? Back on speaking terms, are you?"

She scowled at me. "No. He hasn't spoken to me all week. It should blow over. It usually does."

I half smiled and drained my glass. She did the same. "Want me to go?" I asked.

"Nope. My round. Back in five."

I watched her pick up the ice bucket with the empty bottle stuck back in and head for the bar. I don't know why, but I picked my phone up again and looked up Jason.

His profile didn't show anything other than a picture of him. His broad smile was accented by his dimples, his perfect teeth gleaming in the bright sunlight. I assumed he must have been on holiday when it was taken. There was another person in the picture, but they'd been cropped out, and I couldn't tell if they were male or female. I don't know why I was even wondering.

I jumped when a fresh bottle was plonked on the table and looked up.

"Look who I found all on his lonesome."

Before I had the chance to consider my actions, I sighed. "Oh. Hello again. You here alone?"

Jason smiled and put his drink on the table. "Yeah, for half an hour or so. Just waiting for my mate to join me. Is this your regular?" he asked as he sat down without an invitation. I assumed Haylie had already done that before they got here.

"Sort of, yeah," I muttered, glaring at Haylie.

She shrugged and poured more drinks. "We come here every Friday unless one of us has other plans. Are you meeting a girlfriend or a boyfriend?" she asked him conversationally.

I wanted to throttle her.

"Colleague," he said, not taking his eyes off me. "Are you celebrating again?"

"Nat's new job," Haylie announced. "New company, she walked the interview last month, so we were celebrating that last time we saw you. Tonight, we're celebrating her new boss not being a tool."

He glanced at her and laughed. "That's always worth celebrating." He took a sip from his bottle then looked back at me. "What do you do?"

I opened my mouth to answer, but Haylie cut me off. "She's a Senior Finance Administrator, but she took a pay cut and demotion to work closer to home."

I clenched my teeth and shook my head as he frowned and asked, "Why would you do that?"

"Because," I began, more loudly than was probably necessary, "the commute was killing me, and the pay cut doesn't leave me that much out of pocket after fuel."

He raised his chin as if seeing the logic in my decision and took another sip.

"What do you do, Jason?" Haylie chimed.

"I'm an engineer."

"Oh, interesting. Mechanical or electrical?"

I don't know what my face did, but judging by Jason's smile it must have amused him. I glared at her and asked, "What the hell do you know about engineering?"

"Enough," she replied, looking intently in his direction.

"Water and gas," he went on. "It's pretty boring, really. I handle burst pipes and stuff like that." I noticed he'd relaxed some, dropping the formality of his new accent.

Haylie continued her questioning. "In the area or...?"

"Since I know the area, I stay here when I need to come on a job up this way," he explained. "What about you, Haylie? What do you do?"

I sat quietly, watching their interaction as she explained her job as a support worker for adults with learning disabilities. He seemed genuinely interested and fully engaged as she spoke, drinking and chatting as though they were old friends.

I supposed for the most part, they were. Or had been until he left for uni. Haylie had slated him more than anyone for how he'd handled *that*. She spent two years swearing to castrate him if she ever saw his face again. That wasn't likely, though. A few weeks after he left, his mum put her house on the market and moved down south with her new boyfriend. No one expected him to turn up here again. He had no reason to.

I slumped back in my seat and drank while Haylie quizzed him on his job, apparently I'd been forgotten by them both. I didn't mind. I was about to make an excuse to hide in the toilets when she jumped up. "Need a piss."

What I thought was *bollocks*. What I said was, "Nice. Stay classy, Hayles."

Jason laughed, turning his attention back to me. He pulled a mobile out of his back pocket and shook it at me. "So, you really don't want to be friends, eh?"

I pressed my lips together and raised my eyebrows.

"Look, I just want to have a drink. Talk it out, clear the air. Can we at least do that? I just want to apologize."

"There's nothing to apologize for."

He gave me a disbelieving look, one brow arched slightly. "No? Come on, Nat, just one drink."

I sighed. He was putting in quite some effort, and it wouldn't hurt me to give him half an hour of my time. Anyway, I was curious what sort of excuse he was going to give me for what he did. "Fine, one drink. Coffee, tomorrow afternoon. Here."

He looked around the bar, his eyes focusing on someone by the door. He raised his hand, one finger extended. I didn't turn to look at who had arrived. "Can I get your number?" he asked, looking back at me.

I frowned.

Holding up both hands, he said, "Okay, since you saw my friend request, you know how to reach me through the app if you want. I'll be here at two."

I didn't say anything. It was an effort to even nod.

Draining his bottle, he stood up. "Tomorrow then. Have a great night. I'm glad your boss isn't a tool."

I smiled. "See you tomorrow."

I picked up my glass and drank the lot, not wanting to watch him go. I glanced up and watched his arse in those ridiculously well-fitting jeans as he walked toward the exit. A large group came in the other door as he passed, so I didn't get a look at who he was meeting, but whoever it was clearly wasn't set on drinking here.

"Has he fucking run off again?" Haylie demanded, wiping her hands on her jeans. She apparently didn't bother to dry them in her hurry to get back to quizzing my ex-boyfriend.

"He had to go. His friend arrived."

"Did you see him?" she asked, sitting down and grasping her glass. "Was he fit?"

"How do you know it was a bloke?" I questioned, glancing at his empty bottle. "Women are engineers too, you know."

"Piss off. How many women do you know who crawl about in holes to fix burst pipes for a living?"

It was a pointless argument, so I conceded and checked the contents of the bottle. "Another?"

"No. I think we should get the fuck out of here since it stopped raining."

I knew what she was thinking. She could try. It was a big city, but I was almost certain she could track him down. "Okay. Where to?"

She pursed her lips and tweaked them to the side. "Mambo's."

I shook my head.

"Come on, Nat. You love karaoke."

I sighed and finished my drink. "Fine. It's only nine though. Do not put me in for anything I don't usually sing without a few jaegers."

Her grin was stupid. I knew what that meant.

## CHAPTER FOUR

My head was pounding, and my mouth felt like it was full of sand. I didn't want to focus on how it tasted. Instead I turned over, and my arm hit a body next to mine. That was bad.

Worse. The body was completely naked. I knew because when they turned over, an arm and leg pinning me to the bed, both were bare.

I tried to roll away, but I was stuck, and I needed the loo.

"Hay."

Nothing. Not even a grunt.

"Come on, Hayles, let me up before I piss the bed."

"Piss on me, and I'll piss on you right back," she grumbled as she rolled away.

I sat up carefully, adjusted my boobs, tucking them back in my bra, and moved as quickly as my headache would allow to the bathroom.

I sat down and kicked off my knickers, then unhooked my bra and stretched. "What time is it?" I croaked, remembering the pounding I'd given my vocal chords in the karaoke bar.

"One."

I closed my eyes and scratched my head as I yawned. "What are we doing today?"

"Gym."

"Pfft."

I tried to clean my teeth, but started retching and gave up, stepping into the bath and turning on the shower instead. I yelped at the cold water, then stepped fully underneath it, letting the warming drops continue the process of removing my makeup. My pillow had already made a start, I was sure.

It wasn't until I was rubbing shampoo into my hair when I remembered. "Oh, holy shit. Haylie, I'm meeting Jase at two."

She was at the bathroom door in seconds. "What?"

"Coffee, two, The Cross," I spluttered, rinsing the shampoo out of my hair in a panic. "He'll be expecting me to stand him up…"

"Why didn't you tell me this? Shit. Get dried, I'll get your clothes."

I usually take a little bit more care, but I rinsed my hair, scrubbed my face with soap, and was out of that shower in under a minute, and then I forced myself to be brave and clean my teeth.

"I'm not sure I'm fit to drive," I said, padding into the bedroom wrapped in a towel to see Haylie deliberating between a tea dress and a skirt. "Jeans."

"You can't wear jeans, and you'll be fine driving now… it's only two miles."

"I can't wear that fucking dress. I was eight pounds lighter when I bought that," I snapped, reaching past her and grabbing a hanger I knew had my old Bowie tee and ripped jeans on it. "It's coffee, not a date."

She was still stark naked, standing with one hand on her hip. She was the same height as me but slimmer. Her perky, little boobs made me slightly sick with jealousy, as did the floral tattoo that ran the length of her side and over her shoulder, merging with the sleeve that covered her arm. "No? Why are you panicking about being late then?"

I could have answered, I just didn't have the time. Instead, I rubbed myself down with the towel and hunted for some underwear before getting dressed and rubbing furiously at my hair to get most of the water out. Haylie got back into my bed.

"What are you doing about your hair?" she asked, snuggling back in.

I didn't answer, instead I brushed it through and tied it up on top of my head. "I won't be long."

She waved at me, and I ran out the room and down the stairs.

I managed to grab my bag and keys without dropping anything, and slipped on a pair of trainers before running out the door.

\* \* \*

*Can't get parked. I'm on my way.*

I hadn't wanted to contact him, but I didn't want him to think I was petty enough to stand him up. By the time I got to the bar, I was more than flustered, and I knew I looked like hell. It was probably better that way, I decided. If I didn't make an effort, he'd know I wasn't interested.

He was sitting by the window when I walked inside. I took a minute to get myself together and ordered myself a drink before I went to the table, the coffee mug rattling on its saucer in my shaking hands.

It didn't help that he was staring at his phone. I could see what he was looking at over his shoulder. Me. He got my message and was looking at my profile. Stalker.

He was wearing a white t-shirt and he looked tense, his shoulder muscles visible through his top. His hair was pushed back, held there with what I assumed to be a shit ton of wax, and he was resting his head on two fingers, elbow on the chair arm.

Summoning every ounce of courage I could, I said, "Hiya."

He looked up immediately, that smile knocking me sideways. Bastard.

He shoved his phone into his pocket as he got up. "Nat. You look… Thanks for… Umm…"

I sat down and put my mug down in front of me. "I look hungover."

He pulled a face. "A bit… Have you eaten?"

I shook my head and breathed in the scent of the coffee. "I'm okay."

He sat opposite me and picked up his own mug, but didn't drink. "Thanks for coming."

I looked at him over the rim of my mug as I sipped the hot, black, life-giving liquid and tried not to groan at how good it felt. "Don't mention it."

He watched me for a moment, seemingly unsure of what to say to me.

"Are we going to sit here and stare at each other, or do you have something you want to get off your chest?" I asked.

His brows pulled in, but he didn't speak.

"Because I have other things to do," I added.

"I just wanted to talk. See how you've been. Catch up."

I took another sip of coffee, giving him a sceptical look. "Like old friends? I don't remember parting on friendly terms, Jase."

"I just wanted to… Well, the way I just left was…" He paused and took a breath. "What I mean is, I shouldn't have vanished like I did. It wasn't fair to you. I wasn't thinking. I was stupid, and it was… Well, it was…"

His fluctuating nervousness gave me a little kick of confidence, and I put the mug down. "It was a shitty thing to do, Jase. You didn't even manage to dump me by text. You just vanished. You ghosted me before it even had a name."

He looked at his hands. The spark of confidence grew, and before I knew what I was saying I added, "Do you know what that shit does to an eighteen-year-old girl?"

He didn't, he couldn't possibly. It wasn't a fair question, but it wasn't a fair situation. He wanted to see me, he'd put himself in the firing line. "You ruined my confidence, Jase. You took that from me when I needed it most, and the fight to get it back—"

"I made a mistake," he said, cutting me off.

"Yeah." I picked up my mug, sat back, and sipped my coffee, watching him. "You did."

He was quiet for a minute. Maybe two. Then he broke the tense silence by asking, "So, how've you been?"

I shrugged. No way was I getting into that. Not with him.

"You said you're in admin?" he enquired.

I nodded once.

"Married?" he pressed.

My answer was reluctant. "Divorced."

"Kids?"

I couldn't stop the bitter sniff. "No. None of that particular baggage, thankfully."

I saw his eyebrows pull in slightly and his head jerk back just a fraction before his features smoothed out and he smiled. "You look well."

I really did laugh, then. "Wow."

He gave me a confused look. "What?"

"That's a very polite way of telling me I gained weight. I was already aware, but, you know… Thanks."

He looked horrified. "Is it? No. That's not what I was… Jesus, Nat, don't you take compliments at all anymore?"

"They've been thin on the ground," I responded, glancing out the window. "You left me. That wasn't really much of a compliment, was it? Then my marriage ended… Well, there weren't many compliments there, either. To be honest, I can't remember the last time anyone gave me one so no, I don't suppose I do."

When I glanced back at him, he looked wounded. I don't know why, but guilt pricked at me. "Okay, that wasn't fair… I'm sorry, Jase, but I don't know what I'm here for. I don't think there's anything left to say. I shouldn't have come."

Something changed in him. He sat up straighter and his obvious awkwardness vanished. "You came because you wanted to see me."

He said this with such confidence, I was forced to pay closer attention. I gave him ten out of ten for bravado. He wasn't far off, however much I hated to admit it. I sipped my coffee.

"You wanted to talk to me three weeks ago, but didn't know what to say. You would have spoken to me last night if Haylie hadn't been there. You're here now for the same reason I am." He watched me for a second, then looked over at the bar. "Excuse me while I order another drink. Do you want another one?"

I shook my head, confused. One second, he was walking on eggshells, then he was all confidence and telling me what was, and then he was walking away. I looked across the room to watch him order, his words going around in my head.

By the time he returned, I was more than halfway through my drink and looking out of the window. It was almost three, and the bar was getting busy, the noise level increasing as groups gathered around us and drinks began flowing. He didn't seem too bothered and picked up exactly where he'd left off.

"You're here, Nathalie, because you have questions you need answered."

"Do I?" I asked with a small laugh. "Such as?"

He leaned forward, holding my gaze. "Why did it feel like that when you realized it was me?"

My mouth suddenly felt parched. He couldn't possibly know what I felt when I saw him. Could he? How did he know my body responded to him as it had the last time we were together? Was he guessing? Had I not managed to hide it? "I don't know what you're talking about."

He sat back in his seat and chewed at his thumbnail, watching me intently. My cheeks heated, not because of what he'd just called me out on, but because of how he was looking at me. Like he still knew me. Like he intended to get to know the parts of me that had changed. I was frozen. I couldn't move. His eyes didn't leave mine, and panic constricted my chest. I took a deep, shaky breath.

He clearly recognized it all. I could tell by his expression that he remembered how my breathing would change when I was nervous. Or excited. He smirked and looked away, picking up his drink. "Will you have dinner with me?"

The change in topic confused me. "What?"

"Dinner, tomorrow."

My brain screamed *no. No, no, no.*

My mouth moved. "Why?"

"To satisfy the curiosity."

Then, of all the stupid questions to follow up with, I asked, "Where?"

There was triumph in his smile. I was furious with myself. "The Plaza. Eight o'clock."

It went against every shred of judgment I had, but he was right. I wanted to know why. I wanted to know why I felt this way when he was close. I wouldn't be surprised to learn that it meant I was a complete idiot, but the least he owed me was dinner and some sort of explanation after the shit he pulled. "Okay."

He looked surprised. "Great. Shall I pick you up?"

I shook my head and put my mug on its saucer. "No. I'll drive. I have work Monday morning, so I can't drink."

He nodded, a small smile playing at the corners of his mouth.

"I have to go. I only put an hour and a half on my parking ticket," I said, getting up.

He stood up and grinned, his azure eyes searching my face. "Thank you."

"Yeah. Well, I'll see you tomorrow."

I gave him a brief smile and went to step around him, but he blocked my path and leaned forward, brushing his lips against my cheek. He stayed there, so close I could smell his aftershave, feel the few days growth of stubble across his jaw. My breath caught in my throat as I waited for him to say something. He took a breath, and a tingle ran down my neck and spine. I wanted to turn my head and look at him, but I daren't.

"Thank you, Nathalie," he murmured at last, his voice low in my ear. "I'll make it up to you, I promise."

I took a step forward, and he moved aside. I took another and another, gripping my handbag with both hands as I made my way out of the bar and onto the safety of the street.

I joined the crowd, weaving in and out, lost in my thoughts. I shouldn't have agreed to dinner. I shouldn't have agreed to coffee, which had led to dinner. I didn't want to know why I felt the way I did when I was with him. We were different people now. Yeah, I still held that grudge, but it wasn't a demon I needed to exorcise. The whole experience served as a lesson, one I should have learned a long before I actually did. With my headache clearing, I checked my phone then pressed the call button twice.

"Get up."

Haylie groaned. I waited. Eventually, she asked, "What… Why?"

"Get your shit together, we'll make the gym."

"Coffee was that bad?" she asked, waking herself up.

"Worse. I'll pick you up, just borrow some of my spare gym clothes and throw some in a bag for me. They're in the middle drawer."

"For fuck's sake."

I smirked when she hung up on me.

I took a detour, visiting a small deli for a couple of salads before I went to my car. I arrived with five minutes left on my ticket, threw my bags onto the passenger seat, and fastened my seatbelt, but didn't start the engine. Instead, I rested my forehead against the steering wheel and took a few breaths. Why had I done that? Was I just punishing myself? Did I really want to revisit the past? I didn't think I did, but the thought of seeing him again was already sending a flutter of excitement spreading through my stomach. "Shit."

Pulling myself together, I started the car and backed out of my space. Windows down, I turned the radio up and started singing along as I rolled out of the car park. Another car roared into life on my left, and I was sure I caught sight of Jase, but it was moving too fast. The car followed me out, and I caught a glimpse in my rearview mirror as it turned in the opposite direction to me. There was no way that was him. Not driving that. I was no expert, but a BMW i8 was easily a one hundred and twenty grand car. Engineers didn't drive those things.

## CHAPTER FIVE

*H*aylie looked like shit. I didn't feel fantastic either, but I knew the workout would help.

We'd stopped for a drink and a rest, she leaned against the wall at the back of the gym where we attended our kettlebell class. She didn't really like it, but she'd joined to lend me some support when my physiotherapist suggested I try it. I loved it. It helped me build enough strength where I didn't have to attend physio appointments anymore, and the exercise made me feel good. For a short time, at least.

"Who goes out for dinner on a Sunday night?"

"Someone who doesn't want to end up drinking too much and doing something stupid."

She looked at me with her brows raised. "If you really hate him so much, why agree to meet him a second time?"

I scowled at her and took a long drink of water.

"Unless you're planning to get him out of your system properly."

I almost choked. "That is not what—"

"Why else would he invite you to a hotel? He wants to get into your pants for old times' sake. Bet you." She wiggled her brows over her water bottle then lowered it slowly. "Unless… oh, my god. Are you after scratching that itch?"

I looked at her in horror. "Absolutely not!"

"So, you admit to the itch?" she asked smugly.

"No."

She rolled her eyes. "Ugh. Why else would you go to the trouble?"

"I…" I didn't have an answer. I could see how she'd come to that conclusion, but I was certain the very last thing on my mind was jumping in the sack with him. I didn't want to be in bed with anyone, except her when she couldn't get her drunken arse home of course. She was the exception. She hadn't betrayed me, hurt me, broken my heart. Not yet, anyway. There was still time. I never ruled anything out. "He wants to make it up to me. I don't know how he plans to do that, but it's costing me nothing to let him try. It might even help me get over it, it's been long enough."

It was only there for a second, the look of pity, but I saw it. She covered it by saying, "Whatever. Just tell him if he hurts you again I'll string him up by the balls."

I stared after her as she went back to her exercise space to resume the session. I didn't know what she wanted from me. I walked away the first time I saw him. I was happy to let him pass through without so much as a conversation. She invited him to sit with us at the bar. She instigated his presence in my life, not me.

"What are you wearing?" she asked, breathless as the workout resumed.

"I don't know. I hadn't thought about it."

"Dress. Definitely wear *that* dress." I ignored her. She carried on. "You need to wow him."

"I do not. It's dinner, it's him trying to make up for something that slaughtered my confidence. He won't manage it, but I get a free dinner while watching him squirm. I won't see him again after tomorrow."

"You reckon?"

"Yes. I'm certain." I knew she would have called bullshit if she could breathe. Thankfully, she was knackered and had to concentrate hard on not smashing herself in the face with her kettlebell.

\* \* \*

We ate our warm salads in the car outside her house. I dodged any more talk of Jase, and when I finally got her to leave, I went home and ran a bath. I loved a good workout, but they left me aching. It was a good ache, it meant everything was working, but I couldn't sleep with it. I didn't think I was going to sleep much anyway with today's events spinning around in my head, but the bath was supposed to help.

I laid there soaking when I heard a notification alert on my phone. I reached for it and opened the app to see it was Jason. His friend request was still there, staring at me. I'd just put the thing down when another came in. I turned it back on to find a message in the app.

*Still not friends then?*

I looked at the message for a minute. Could we be?

**Not yet. No.**

I saw three little dots bouncing at the bottom of the screen and waited.

*So, we could be?*

**Maybe.**

He sent back a fist bump emoji, and despite being pissed off at him I laughed, closing the app. It was strange, but I wasn't anxious about the following night. He'd been quite intense in the bar earlier, but just then he seemed more like the Jason I remembered. I knew that wasn't possible. He wasn't the same person he'd been back then. Neither of us were.

I supposed that meant I should give him the benefit of the doubt. He wasn't the same guy any more than I was the girl he ran out on. People changed. Didn't they?

The possibility of him being different now brought tears to my eyes. It was years ago, but it hurt like it was yesterday. Did he really feel remorse for what he'd done? He sounded sincere enough. There was no other reason for him to be chasing me, begging for my forgiveness. I believed our meeting was one of chance. There was no way he could know I'd be there that night, was there? Nobody was that weird.

More memories, ones I'd kept buried for years, surfaced to remind me that yes, they could. People did some weird shit when they got stupid ideas in their heads. I'd seen just how crazy it could get first hand. I dropped the phone and sank beneath the water. You can't cry under water, and I was done crying. I'd cried enough over Jase and every bad decision I'd made since. I'd decided to see him again, I wasn't going to cry over it until there was something to cry about, and so far, all he'd done was promise to earn forgiveness and make me smile.

When I was out of air, I sat up and wiped the water from my face. My phone was going nuts.

I picked it up and without thinking, accepted the incoming video call.

"What's up?" I asked, expecting to see Haylie's face. My eyes widened slightly as I looked directly at Jason's amused face.

"You're definitely coming tomorrow?"

My wet hair was hanging in tails around my face and it was obvious I was in the bath. I stared at the screen.

"Jase... I'm a bit busy."

He appeared to be a laid on a bed, the white sheets behind him showing the bright blue of his eyes. There was a small smile tugging at his mouth. "I can see that. Are you still joining me tomorrow?"

I couldn't believe what he was asking. He'd video called me for that? "Really?"

"Really, what?"

"Are you this needy? Are you going to check every," I did the math in my head, "four hours to make sure I don't stand you up?"

He looked thoughtful then smiled, raising his brows. "I wasn't going to, but that's an excellent idea."

I sighed and wiped a few drops of water from my face. "I should have never accepted your message."

"But you did, so now I can keep checking in," he said grinning.

"If I turn off my phone you'll just have to sweat it out, won't you?"

He shrugged, and I noticed the beautifully tanned skin of his muscled shoulder come into view. He'd filled out considerably over the years, in a good way, and he obviously worked out.

"I'm going now."

"You don't have to."

"I'm not dressed for company."

"You're not dressed at all, Nat. You're in the bath."

My cheeks heated, and I almost groaned when I saw the evidence in the tiny video call window and watched him studying my face. "Goodbye, Jason."

"Tomorrow?" There was genuine hope in his voice.

I closed my eyes briefly, sighed, and gave him a stiff smile. "Yes. Tomorrow."

He was smirking when I ended the call. I took a second to memorize some of his features. The new ones. The few lines in the corners of his eyes that accompanied the dimples in his cheeks. His thicker brows. The curve of his mouth when he smiled. And he was gone.

I looked at the phone for a second, and then turned it off before dropping it and getting out of the bath. I sat down to dry my hair, smiling to myself. He was turning out to be a complete pain in the arse. I didn't want him messaging and calling me. I had declined his invitation for that very reason.

I made short work of my hair, I was exhausted and needed some sleep. While I fully intended to be home by ten the following night, I suspected it would end up being a late one. He'd proven he could get me talking whether I wanted to or not. Twice.

I turned my phone back on when I got into bed and set it to silent. I had a message waiting from Haylie and two from Jason.

*Remember to wow him. I want all the gossip Monday morning. Text me.*

I grinned, shook my head and turned off the lamp, replying with three kisses. Then I opened his.

*I set my alarm for eleven and three. Speak to you soon.*

*Wow. You really turned it off. Tomorrow it is then.*

I almost replied but thought better of it. Placing it screen down on my bedside table, I turned over and cuddled into my duvet. It didn't matter if I was making a mistake. It was too late. He'd pulled me in expertly. If I hadn't seen the look on his face when he first saw me I'd have sworn it was all planned. But he was as shocked as I was. And he'd felt it, whatever this pull is between us, just as I did. He told me he had. Whatever happened, I had to find out. With my luck, it was going to end badly, but that wasn't enough to stop me. Not now.

## CHAPTER SIX

He was at the bar when I walked in. I didn't need him to turn around to know it was him. The cut of his jeans, the way the shirt hung on his frame, the way the light made his brown hair shine. The sight of him almost undid the work I'd done to present myself as calm and confident.

I approached the bar and saw he was smiling into the mirrored back wall that displayed the various spirits on offer. I hopped up onto the barstool beside him and waited for him to acknowledge me.

"And a prosecco," he said to the barman, still looking at me through the mirror. "You made it."

"I said I would."

He turned his head and smiled. "You look lovely."

I'd chosen a dress, not the one Haylie suggested, but it had a low enough neckline to show off some cleavage while still being comfortable, and flat, black pumps. Nothing too fancy, I didn't want to look as though I were really trying. "You scrub up all right yourself."

My drink was served, and I thanked him, waiting for him to move away from the bar.

When he didn't, I took a sip of my drink to help with my nerves and said, "You asked all about me but didn't tell me anything about you."

"Not a lot to tell," he responded, turning to face me, leaning on the bar. His eyes flicked over me, then settled on my face. "I went to uni, graduated, started working, and here I am."

I crossed one foot over the other and put my left arm over my stomach. "Evasive."

He laughed. "Okay. I went to uni, mum sold the house and moved down there with her now husband. I settled down south since that's where she was. I got a job, and got married, which didn't work out. I work away a lot, so I live in hotels most of the time. I was needed up here, so I've been back and forth quite a bit recently. I was out with a colleague after work when I bumped into you. Is that better?"

I played with the stem of my glass. "Much. Sorry your marriage didn't work out."

He shrugged. "Shit happens. We're still friends."

My brows rose. "Really?"

"Yeah. Was yours a difficult split?"

I laughed without much humor. I couldn't disguise my bitterness at the whole mess. "You could say that, yeah. I'd go as far as to say painful. But it's been years now. Seven. Haven't seen him since…" I trailed off, not wanting to share that small detail. "But like you said, shit happens."

I don't know what he saw in my eyes, but he clearly didn't like it. I saw a muscle tic along his jaw as he clenched his teeth. Then he took a mouthful of whatever he was drinking. It looked like vodka and tonic.

"So," I said, taking a breath in. "Are we eating at the bar?"

He brightened immediately. "No, I booked a table. Shall we go through?"

I slid from the stool and was surprised when he grasped my free hand. My instinct was to flinch away, but I forced myself not to react. He was being friendly. I was in a safe place. He wouldn't hurt me.

Instead, I answered, "Yeah, I'm starving."

\* \* \*

Dinner was amazing. I stuck to water after that first glass of prosecco, and despite my insistence he have wine with his meal, he did the same. He kept the conversation general, and I hated to admit that I'd enjoyed his company. I discovered he spent time in the gym to pass the evenings, he was amazed at how I used kettlebells to help with a back problem, at least that's how I presented it.

"So, this new job of yours," he said. "How's that going?"

I smiled. "It's great. I'm really enjoying it," I answered honestly. "What about you? How long will you be in the area?"

He shrugged. "I'm in and out. We have an office here, and I come up when I'm needed. There's quite a lot on just now, so I could be in and out for a few weeks."

That made me nervous. The whole dinner thing was supposed to be a one off, but if he was coming back… I pushed my chair back, about to leave the table. "This was nice. Thank you for the invitation."

He stood up, but I was out of my seat before he could get to my side of the table, clutching my bag to my abdomen.

"My pleasure. Thank you for coming. Can I walk you to your car?"

My instinct was to say no, but the way he looked at me with hope made me curious. I shrugged one shoulder. "Yeah. Thanks."

He walked in silence at my side until we reached the lobby, then slowed. I took an extra three steps before I realized he stopped.

"Nathalie, I… I really am sorry for what I did twelve years ago. I handled that so badly. I know it was a long time ago, and I can't change it now, but I just want you to know it ate at me for years. It still does. More so now that I know what it did to you. I'm sorry."

I stopped and turned, surprised to see his expression. He looked as though he were in pain. I remembered what I said to Haylie, but the truth was, seeing him squirm like this was torture.

"Jase…" I paused. My mouth was dry. I wasn't prepared for it, and nerves fluttered in my stomach as I searched for a response. I didn't understand why, but I wanted to comfort him. I wanted to take the pain away. Seeing him so full of regret, so tortured, was hell. Those three paces between us felt like an abyss. My tongue flicked out to wet my bottom lip, and his eyes focused on it as I said, "I can't say it doesn't matter. But… well, I can forgive you. I think."

His eyes searched mine for a second before he moved forward. He moved slowly. Cautiously. His right hand reaching for me, his eyes scanning my face for a sign of rejection. I didn't move. I leaned into his palm as he pressed it gently against my cheek, and closed my eyes as his face came closer to mine.

Our lips touched, his free hand found my waist, and I melted. I'd come here expecting awkwardness and stilted conversation. I'd arrived still feeling bitter but curious, determined to hide my nervousness, fighting not to let him see how terrified I was. But I wasn't terrified now. I didn't fear him. He was still Jase. The feel of his lips against mine was all it took to stir up the feelings I'd kept locked away.

I hadn't wanted to, but I believed him. He'd never meant to hurt me.

I'd hated him. I'd cried and cursed his name a thousand times. I intended to let that be the end of it, to never see him again and be happy about it.

But I was about to leave feeling entirely differently.

"Thank you."

There was so much relief in the two words muttered against my lips, my chest constricted. Then his hand left my cheek, and he stepped back, rubbing the back of his neck.

I caught his other hand as he released my waist and held it for a second, before dropping it and smiling awkwardly.

He was watching my eyes. I didn't look away. I held his gaze for a moment, wondering what I was supposed to say.

"Stay."

"What." I said. It was a reflex, not a question.

Stay. With him. Excitement roiled in my stomach as I took a step forward.

I wanted him. I needed to feel his lips on mine again. I needed him to be my Jason just one last time.

There was no more discussion. He took my hand in his and turned, leading me away from the doors to the right of the check in desk, and toward the lifts.

He hit the call button and the doors opened straight away. I didn't have time to think, his hand settling on the small of my back, guiding me inside.

I turned to ask what he was doing, but the doors were closing, and he was kissing me again. I was kissing him. My hands skimmed over the smooth skin of his face, and his gripped my waist.

Excitement pumped through my body as he kissed me again. This time with more urgency. More passion. I had no choice but to reciprocate, my body responding to him in ways I'd forgotten it could. I was pushed along by a rush of euphoria, his lips teasing mine apart and fueling the fire that was raging through my veins. A fire he'd started. A fire that hadn't warmed me for over a decade.

The doors opened, and he backed up abruptly, taking me by the hand and leading me out and down a hallway.

"Jason."

He stopped with his hand on what I assumed to be the door to his room, his head bowed. "Tell me you don't feel this, that this isn't what you want, and I'll take you to your car."

I couldn't speak. I could barely even think, but I knew my car wasn't where I wanted to be. It was the last place I wanted to be. I'd been denying it, but it was there. Right then it was all I needed.

I squeezed his hand, and he unlocked his door.

He led me inside. The door snapped shut behind me, and I startled. He didn't notice.

The room was shrouded in darkness, but he led me along until the bed nudged at the backs of my knees, and then he guided me down.

His kiss was more urgent. His lips more demanding. His hands roaming.

My skin tingled beneath every brush of his fingers, and I needed more. More of him. With one hand on his shoulder I pushed him back, reaching for his shirt with the other. The buttons unfastened easily, and he shrugged it off as I ran my fingers over his chest.

"Just a minute."

"No…" I gasped, tugging at his shoulder. "Leave the light off. Please."

He was fumbling with something. Then I heard the crinkle of foil before he kissed me, his hands finding mine, fingers lacing and pressing them down next to either side of my head.

"Can I make it up to you?" he asked, pulling away from my mouth and kissing my neck.

I moaned, breath hitching as his tongue traced the hollow of my throat. His kisses resumed, moving down my chest. "Nathalie."

My answer was to wrap my leg around his hip and pull him closer. I felt his erection through his jeans as he ground against me, and I angled my hips up instinctively.

I tried to raise my head, but I was pinned. He released my hands immediately, holding himself above me while I pushed myself up and shuffled further back on the bed.

He stayed where he was. "I can't see."

I chuckled and knelt on the bed, finding his shoulders. "You don't need to."

The low rumble that came from his throat as he found the hem of my dress sent another wave of excitement through me. His agreement came with my dress being dropped on the bed beside me, and his mouth claiming mine.

## CHAPTER SEVEN

He was out cold. I lay with my head on his chest and listened to his breathing for a few minutes, wondering what the time was. The room was still dark, but a few shafts of daylight were breaking through gaps in the curtains. Just enough for me to see.

The answer came with an alarm going off, and I panicked. I was under the duvet, but I was naked, and him awake meant lights. I told myself to calm down. It was too late to run. I didn't really want to. It wasn't as though he was going to call once I left anyway, so I may as well just enjoy these final few minutes with him.

It had been as close to perfect as I could have hoped. He was unusually considerate, from my own experiences, and while I hadn't climaxed, it hadn't been the disappointing experience I'd become used to with other partners. He didn't know I hadn't climaxed since I put on a decent enough act and just enjoyed the closeness. But he didn't need to know. It wasn't his fault, it was just how I was.

I ran my hand over his chest. "Jase. Your phone."

His hand ran up and down my arm, tickling, but he ignored his alarm.

"Don't you have work?"

He moved, turning onto his side to turn off the alarm, and I lifted my head to let him.

"You stayed." Despite it being thick with sleep, there was relief in his voice. I felt a bit bad he expected me to bail as soon as he was out.

"Yeah…" I wrinkled my nose at him. "You fell asleep and, well it was late and this bed's really comfy, so I thought I might as well."

He was smirking at me as he lay on his side, watching me. I wasn't sure what to say. What to do. "What time is it?"

"Probably about eight."

My eyes widened. "What?"

"What's wrong?"

"I'm late… I'm late for work." I clutched the duvet to my chest and sat up, tucking it around me as I tried to work out the best way to get out of the bed, gather up my clothes, and get into the bathroom without him seeing me naked. The room wasn't that light, but I didn't want to chance it.

"Chill out, you won't be that late."

"I can't be late at all. I haven't been there long enough… shit."

His hand brushed the small of my back, and I scooted to the edge of the bed.

"I need to get dressed…"

Sighing, he rolled over and out of bed. I watched him walk over to the window and pull back the curtains, tucking the duvet tighter around myself before he turned around. His body was silhouetted against the bright morning light as my eyes adjusted. Then I got a really good look.

"So, you really workout?"

He looked down at himself then back to me, tilting his head as his eyes met mine again. "A bit."

I laughed, trying not to stare. What ended up happening was my eyes roved over his entire body. He watched me watching him, his right hand behind his neck.

"Want me to stand here a bit longer, or shall I go and get sorted since you're obviously going to hide under that duvet until I leave the room?"

I bit my bottom lip and pulled in my brows. "One more minute."

He was on me in seconds, pushing me down onto the bed and kissing me. I was laughing beneath him, trying hard not to let the duvet slip.

"Jase," I murmured between kisses. "I'm late, and I have to go home and change before I go to work."

"You started it. Can I see you tonight?"

"When do you leave?"

"I was going to head back this evening, but one more night here won't hurt. I can drive back in the morning."

"Your company will love you costing them an extra night."

He laughed and kissed the end of my nose. "Let me worry about that." Then he pushed off the bed and went to the bathroom.

I moved quickly. How my dress was going to look after being fucked on, then slept on, I had no idea, but I found it and my knickers and pulled them on in a haste. The bra came next, and I'd just tugged my dress back over my head when I noticed the notepad and pen on the nightstand. Before I could think better of it, I scribbled down my number.

I was just sliding my feet into my shoes when he came out of the bathroom, holding out his toothbrush.

I looked at it like it was on fire.

"You'll share my bed but not my toothbrush?"

"It's just..." I trailed off, knowing I sounded ridiculous.

"We exchanged enough bodily fluids last night, don't you think?"

I glared at him. "You... you used a... don't tell me you fucking stealthed me."

He gave me a look that made me feel terrible, took my hand, and pushed the toothbrush into it. "Just clean your bloody teeth." Then he walked into the small entrance hall to the hotel room and opened the wardrobe.

I brushed my teeth quickly, making sure to rinse the brush thoroughly when he popped his head around the door. "There. No stealthing."

I choked on the water I was rinsing my mouth with when I looked through the mirror to see him dangling a knotted condom on the end of his index finger.

His eyes were gleaming with mirth. "If you're ready, I'll walk you to your car."

I wasn't sure I was ready. Walking out of this room meant it was over. He'd said he wanted to see me again, but the part of me that didn't believe anything good could possibly happen to me was whispering in my ear. I'd ignored it until then, but faced with drawing a line under our one night, I was forced to listen.

"About tonight..."

He stepped into the bathroom, no sign of the condom, thankfully, and leaned both hands on the sink, trapping me. I looked at him through the mirror, trying desperately not to lock up, and forced a smile.

"Where do you want me to meet you?"

"Why don't you text me when you're ready, and I can pick you up?"

"Nice try."

He shrugged. "Was worth a shot. Really though, we don't have to make any set plans. We can see how we feel later since we both have work."

I relaxed, closed my eyes, and tipped my head back, resting it on his shoulder. I could have stayed longer, part of me really wanted to, but... "I have to go."

He wrapped his arms around my waist and kissed my cheek. "I don't want you to."

I wanted to stay here with him. I wanted to spend as much time with him as I could, but I didn't have the courage to say it. I'd learned too many hard lessons to risk opening myself up again. Especially not to him. "I wrote my number on the pad on your night stand. I finish work at five."

"I know. It's already in my phone." His breath was hot on the shell of my ear, and I had to try hard not to melt against him. I was both relieved and bereft when he stepped away, my back growing cold in his absence. "Come on. I'll walk down with you. I've got a busy day myself."

He took my hand and led me out, grabbing my bag from the unit as we passed. It was odd, but I completely relaxed walking hand in hand with him to the lift. Like this was where I was meant to be. It wasn't true. It wasn't real. It wasn't anything but what it was. My one-night stand walking me to my car to spare me the walk of shame.

When we were locked inside the lift, he turned to look at me. "Thank you."

"For what?"

"Agreeing to see me. I know it must have been… well, hard, but I meant what I said. I do want to make it up to you. And not… well, you staying the night wasn't part of the plan. I wanted to… It wasn't supposed to end up looking like apology sex."

In my head, I was saying he didn't have to. That it was fine. That I hadn't thought last night was about an apology. To go back to his life and forget me like he did before. But what came out of my mouth was, "I'm looking forward to it."

✷ ✷ ✷

I speed walked from my car into the office. I should have run, but I didn't want to draw even more attention to myself. I was surprised to see two blokes in suits sitting on the same chairs I'd sat on when I was waiting for my interview, and wracked my brain to remember what was scheduled for that morning.

"You're—"

"Thanks, Chantal," I snapped as I passed, trying to flash a smile at the two waiting interviewees.

I went straight to my desk and turned on the computer, then rushed into the small kitchen to make myself a cup of coffee. I'd missed breakfast and there was no way I could work without caffeine.

I considered calling in to Tony's office before I started, but thought better of it. While my absence would be reported, I didn't really want to have to give a reason as to why I was so late. I hadn't had time to think up a suitable excuse and there was no way I was telling him the truth.

Just as I reached my desk, mug in shaking hand, his office door opened, and he stepped out. "Nathalie. Is everything all right?"

My face flushed. "Yeah, umm, I overslept. I'm so sorry, Tony, I'll make up the time."

He watched me sit down, and then he bent over so the others couldn't see his face. "Tell you what," he said with a cheeky smile, "go and grab some sandwiches for lunch at eleven thirty and we'll call it covered."

I nodded and beamed gratefully. "Anything specific?"

"Ham salad should be fine. Two please, with cokes."

He straightened, and I noticed he'd left a twenty-pound note on my desk as he turned to greet the first in the line for an interview. With a quiet breath out, I steadied my nerves and started to work my way through the day's emails. It could have gone much worse.

I could feel eyes on me, but I didn't turn around and start explaining myself. I didn't answer to any of them. I didn't fully understand how I'd gotten off so lightly, except Tony did seem like a decent bloke and people screwed up now and then.

The minutes ticked by until it was time for me to leave. It wasn't far to the bakery, and it gave me the opportunity to grab something to eat. I stuffed a roll down in the car before rushing in to deliver Tony his sandwiches, intending to work through my official break to make up the time I'd missed in the morning.

"I got a receipt, and here's your change," I said, holding out my right hand while depositing a plastic bag on his desk. "I'm just going to work through lunch, so those emails all go out on time, and I get on with the extra invoices Cara sent for me."

He didn't get up, but took his change and nodded to the seat opposite him. "There's no need, Nathalie, have a break. This is Jason, one of the other partners. He designed and patented the filtration system and the sealing technology we use here. Jason, this is Nathalie."

I hadn't noticed him sitting there. I'd been so focused on Tony, on making up for my tardiness that morning, that I hadn't considered there'd be anyone else with him in his office. Or why he'd asked for two sandwiches.

Turning to my other boss, I smiled. He was wearing a blue polo shirt with the company logo on his right pec and a pair of dark blue work trousers. "Hi. It's lovely to…"

His eyes were wide, lips slightly parted in a look of shock. He couldn't have been any more shocked than I was, but it was close enough.

"Y-you… why… Excuse me…"

I was out of that office like a shot. Everyone else had left for lunch, and I made my way to the staff toilet. The door was almost shut when a booted foot was wedged in between.

"Nat, listen."

"Move your foot, Jase, or so help me I'll slap you."

"I didn't know you worked here. How would I have known that?"

"It's your fucking company," I hissed, leaning against the door.

"I don't run this office. I'm only here to interview new engineers. Honestly, I didn't know you worked here. You weren't here when I arrived, were you?"

I clenched my teeth and leaned harder against the door, but his steel toe capped boots weren't giving. "No. Because you made me late."

The door was shoved open a fraction and his foot withdrew. My body weight pushing on the door caused it to slam, and I fumbled with the lock. When it was finally secure, I leaned my hands against it and closed my eyes.

His voice came through the door, and I stepped back. "I'll wait outside for you after work. Let me take you for a drink and talk this through. Please."

I shook my head. How was I supposed to spend four and a half hours in this building knowing he was here and concentrate on work? "No."

"I promise you, I didn't know."

I opened the door and stepped out. "Is that why he was okay with me being late? Did you tell him you nailed his receptionist, and she was running home to get changed?"

He was smirking. I was getting annoyed as he said, "No. I left him sitting there looking confused while I chased after you. He's probably coming up with all sorts of mad theories, waiting for me to get back and tell him why I've pissed off his *Business Administrator.*"

"I don't believe this," I muttered, rubbing my index finger over my forehead.

Not looking for permission, he stepped up close and said, "I'll be outside at five. Mine's the white car."

His body was almost touching mine as he looked down at me for a moment.

I didn't say anything. I just stood there, longing to lean into him, feel his arms around me, to ease the anxiety. But I couldn't. If I let him in, if I relied on him for comfort, I'd be a step closer to falling into the trap. I couldn't be sure if I hadn't already, but I didn't move, and I watched him walk out, back toward Tony's, no, their office, then locked myself back in the toilet.

"Shit…"

I looked at myself in the mirror. I looked awful. No makeup. Wearing my Ugg boots, leggings, and a long shirt. My hair was pulled up on top of my head in a messy bun.

"Fuck him. Fuck this."

I was calm and collected when I returned to my desk with coffee. Over the course of the afternoon, people came and went, but I didn't look up from my screen. I didn't move from my seat until everyone except Tony was gone. He didn't bother me, I assumed saving me the embarrassment of that conversation. But by that time, the anger had long since burned out and the shock had worn off. All that was left was a heavy feeling in the pit of my stomach. Jason was waiting for me. I had to face him. I had to listen to whatever bullshit excuse he was going to give me, if only to try and smooth it over for work. I knew what was coming. "I didn't know, Nathalie," and "I don't come to this office often."

But how could he not know?

Was that why he was there that first night? Had he set it all up? Had he read my resume and influenced it all?

I'd have to face him.

It was almost five thirty when I walked out the front door. Three cars were in the carpark. My little three door hatch, Tony's black Audi RS, and a gleaming white BMW i8 with a light blue trim. While I was impressed, I walked toward the thing shaking my head, and he started the engine. I jumped at the sound, not expecting the roar as he revved it, I assumed telling me to hurry up.

I swallowed the bile rising in my throat as I approached, walking around the thing like it was going to bite me. When I finally got in, I took my time closing the door. "This is your car?"

"I treated myself for my birthday."

I didn't look at him, but I could hear the smile in his voice. "Where are we going?"

"I told you, I want to have a drink and explain."

I looked out the window as we passed a fast food drive-through. "Could do that there."

"I'm not doing this in public, Nathalie."

The knot tightened in my stomach. "I don't want to—"

He hit the brakes, and I leaned forward heavily in my seat, the belt cutting into my neck, and looked at him wide-eyed. "Jason! You can't stop in the middle—"

"Why are you frightened?" he demanded, gripping the steering wheel, staring at me.

"I–I'm not."

His voice softened. "Nat… I hear it in your voice. I can see it on your face. Why are you frightened of me?"

"I…" A car horn sounded behind us while my head swam with thoughts. Part of me wanted to scream it at him, but the overriding part, the inner voice that told me not to trust anyone, to never let anyone in because of what they'd do to me, took over. "Just drive. You're causing a scene."

I tried not to show my terror, but the way he pulled away, slowly, suggested I had failed miserably. I didn't need the questions he was obviously going to ask. I didn't know how to give him the answers without ending up a crying mess.

# CHAPTER EIGHT

The room was pristine. No hint of the state we'd left it in that morning. He allowed me inside first, closing the door softly behind him before opening a minibar I hadn't noticed and taking out a lager. "Want one?"

I shook my head and looked around. There was a sofa by the window, a chair by the dresser. I tried not to look at the bed. I couldn't think about how happy I'd been earlier when all I could concentrate on was the disappointment. He'd set me up. He'd given me a job and lured me into bed, I was certain. Growing angry at myself for not working it out, I wanted to get out of here as soon as possible. "Go on, out with it then."

I watched him for a second. He looked conflicted. I expected him to start asking awkward questions, and my heart raced at the prospect of answering them. I wasn't ready.

"Please, sit down."

I raised my eyebrows as he tipped the bottle in the direction of the sofa.

"Or stand there and glower at me, whatever." He took a swig of his drink. "I've only been to the office up here four times," he began. "I come to interview engineers since I'm the engineering guy, to clean up if I worked nearby, or to drop off equipment. I don't have anything to do with hiring admin staff, that's Cara's job. Tony handles the general business side of things, Rich deals with the samples. I'm based down in Cambridgeshire." He pointed at the window. "I knew there was a new member on the admin team, I knew Cara came up to interview you. I didn't read your application or even get your name because it's not what I deal with. I had no idea you worked for the company."

"You," I corrected. "I work for you."

He shook his head and sighed. "I only own a quarter of the company, none of us solely employs anyone. More to the point, I don't give a shit who works in the offices if the paperwork gets done. With that in mind, I don't want this to come between us."

"I didn't know there was an 'us.' Regardless, I can't see you anymore." It was out of my mouth before the tears could form in my eyes. He was shaking his head as I continued, "I can't sleep with my boss. It was complicated enough without this, Jase. I can't…"

The tears fell. I wasn't sure why I was crying. Disappointment? Shame? Anger at myself for letting it happen in the first place? All the above, with a healthy dose of concern over how it would look, was probably a fair assessment. But the overriding emotion was fear. I thought I was masking that one well.

"What are you so scared of?"

My heart stopped. "I… I'm not."

He put the bottle down and walked toward me. "Nat, you're scared. I told you I can see it in your eyes, your body language, even hear it your voice. I know I hurt you, and I promised to make it up to you, but I can't do that if you won't tell me the truth, and if you're going to push me away."

I was frozen. My head was a myriad of thoughts, my body tingling with the mix of emotional responses I was having, and it was all too much. I was still crying. There were only inches between us, and I lowered my eyes, focusing on my hands as I picked at my fingernails.

"Look at me."

I shook my head.

"I'm trying to make up for what I did. I want to… You finally let me in, Nat, and... I can't get this right if you won't tell me what I'm doing wrong."

I wanted to. I wanted to look him in the eyes and tell him what had happened. What I needed, everything I wanted, but the fear of what he could do to me was crushing. My hands were trembling, the tears were streaming silently down my face, and I couldn't look up.

He stepped away, backing right up to the vanity. I watched his feet, wondering what he was doing, then his voice broke the tense silence that filled the room. "I'm not keeping you here. If you want to leave, please." I managed to lift my chin and saw him raise a hand and gesture to the door. "I wanted to talk. I wanted to make this right, but I don't want to scare you. The one thing I never wanted to do was hurt you again, but that's what seems to be happening. I can drive you home or get the reception staff to call you a taxi and charge it to me. I won't be back here for a few weeks. I'll give you a heads up when I have to be in town and stay out of your way when I'm at the office."

Swallowing, I crossed the room and made for the door. He didn't speak. I kept my eyes focused on the light wood. On the silver handle. On getting out of this room.

Once I was out of here I could go back to my life. Go back to a world without Jason Locksley. Without wondering when he would vanish. When he would drop me. I was safer on my own. I could live through any physical pain, that was easy enough, but the cracks were still there from the emotional damage I'd lived through, and I knew I couldn't get through it again. He could break me without even trying.

But he was the only person who had come close to fixing me.

I could be myself when I was with him. He made me happy. It had been brief, but it had been real. I believed him when he said it wasn't apology sex. I believed him when he said he wanted to try and make it up to me. I wanted to believe he was a good guy.

I reached for the door handle but stopped. The world had been just a little bit brighter when I walked out of that hotel less than nine hours before.

I had a snap decision to make.

"I'm not frightened of you, Jason. Not the way you think."

He didn't say anything. I turned and leaned against the door. His face was a mask of calm, but his eyes... He was ready to let me walk away. I knew I had to give him something. He needed to hear more than what I'd given him so far. He deserved to hear the truth, however ugly it was.

"When you went—" My voice hitched, and I blinked back tears, trying to compose myself. The strength had come from somewhere, and I was clinging to it. "When you left. No explanation. I was here thinking something awful had happened to you. I went to your mum's house, and she wasn't in. Your phone just rang out. None of your mates would speak to me. Nobody would tell me where you were. It was two weeks before I finally got a hold of Jackie, and she told me you'd gone to university and wouldn't be back. The next week her house was for sale."

He hung his head. "I thought the distance would—"

"It didn't matter what you thought. You didn't tell me. So, I brushed myself off and went to college. That's all I did. It took Haylie six months to get me out of the house. When she finally managed it, I got wasted and fell into the first pair of arms that wanted me. I didn't know he didn't really love me. You claimed to have loved me and you left. He stayed. I thought it was proof. I thought it was enough."

"I'm—"

"Don't apologize. It wasn't your fault. You asked, I'm telling you what happened and why I'm... Why I'm the way I am. I can't go through the pain again. I can't live knowing I'm not good enough to be... I'd rather be on my own than live through it again. Does that make sense?"

He nodded his head. "I didn't know what to do. I was going away. I had to go to uni. I didn't want to leave you, but I didn't know how often I could come back. I was going to hurt you regardless and didn't know how to handle it, so I ran away from it."

It wasn't what I wanted to hear, but I could tell it was the truth.

"That's how I know leaving right now won't fix anything, Nat. I promise you I didn't know you worked for us. I'd have told you I co-owned the company if I had."

"Why didn't you tell me anyway?"

"That I own one of the fastest growing companies in the country? I've done all right, Nat, but I don't like... Well, I don't shout about it because money attracts the wrong sort of attention."

"You thought I'd—"

I didn't like the look in his eyes. "No. Not you. I know you wouldn't care if I flipped burgers. I did through uni, actually," he said with a wry smile. "Best job I ever had."

"I didn't mean to... I'm just trying to protect myself. I don't have anyone else, Jase. I have to look out for myself. Trusting people ends... Well, experience taught me it ends badly."

He watched me, but stayed where he was. I wasn't sure what to do. Seconds before I'd been leaving. Seconds before I wanted to leave, but that had changed. Right then I wanted to go to him, to tell him it was all right. That it wasn't his fault. The sadness and guilt etched on his face was enough to reduce me to tears again. "You can trust me."

I shook my head. "It's not that simple. I... I can't explain. Not now." I glanced back at the door. "Not here. I shouldn't have come."

His eyes hardened, as he stated, "I disagree." My eyes were drawn to the hand he held out to me. "Don't leave."

I looked back at the door. I absolutely should go.

If I stayed, he'd kiss me. If he kissed me, I'd be lost.

I took a step toward him. He was all I'd really wanted since the day he left me.

Another step. Then one more.

Before I had chance to talk myself out the door I was in his arms. One hand cradled the back of my head, the other took my waist and pulled me close, his face buried in my neck. I closed my eyes as he took a deep breath.

"You won't regret it, I promise."

I took his shoulders and pushed him back, holding him away from me. "Don't make promises. You can't keep them."

His eyes lit up. There was hint of the Jason I used to know in that defiant grin, the younger, cockier Jase who didn't give a shit who he was talking to. He knew what he wanted and knew how to get it. "Watch me."

I'd have laughed if he hadn't kissed me. But it wasn't just a kiss. There was so much said in the way his lips moved against mine than he could have expressed verbally. I'd heard all of it before, but this time, it felt different. He really thought we had a chance. I could tell in the way he touched me. How he closed his eyes to kiss me. He believed it wholeheartedly. I didn't have the courage to believe it myself, but there was a flicker of excitement in my stomach as he backed me toward the bed.

"I promise I won't ever do anything to hurt you again. Never intentionally," he murmured as his kisses left my mouth and moved to my neck. He sucked gently on my pulse point, and a rush of euphoria trickled down my spine. Instinctively I arched into him, and his hand slid up my shirt, fingers pressing into the soft flesh of my waist.

His mouth was tracing my collarbone, one hand moving from my waist up my back, and the other brushing my jawline, as he whispered, "I just want to make you happy. I want you to feel the way I do when I'm with you."

I wasn't sure what I was feeling right then, but it was as close to happy as I could probably get. "Jase... I... I want to try... I do, I'm just... I'm scared..."

He pulled away, his eyes searching mine. "You don't need to be. Not of me. You want me to stop, I'll stop. You want me to go, I'll go. Whatever makes you happy, Nathalie. All I care about is that. You. I'm just asking for a chance."

I kissed him. I kissed him the way he deserved to be kissed, and he reciprocated with more enthusiasm than I could have imagined. He unbuttoned my shirt as his tongue danced with mine, igniting something in me I believed was long dead. When I was free of my shirt, he unhooked my bra, and let it slide to the ground before he moved his mouth toward my chest. He kissed straight down between my breasts and dropped to his knees to remove my leggings. And that was when I wrapped my arms around myself and froze.

"What's wrong?"

"Turn the light off."

He looked up at me, and I shook my head. It was a stupid request. It was still daylight, and the curtains were open. "Please."

"What don't you want me to see?"

"I… nothing. I just prefer the light off."

He sat back on his heels, looking up at me, and then reached out a hand. His finger traced a line over the black fabric covering my waist. "I felt them last night. A few scars won't scare me off."

He didn't know how bad it looked. Feeling and seeing were two very different experiences. I couldn't look at them, and I'd lived with them for seven and a half years. I swallowed hard and dropped my arms to my sides, watching him kneel back up and kiss my tummy. That was a problem, too. I hadn't managed to lose the weight I'd gained. I hadn't realized I was so conscious of it until that moment.

His fingers were beneath the band of my leggings. "I want all of you. The scars. The nerves. The smiles." As he slid them down my waist, I closed my eyes and held my breath, waiting for his reaction to the deep purple lines that mapped my lower abdomen and hips. Some were inches long, others were small, circular markers of where the pins had been placed to fuse my pelvis back together. The breath was released with a small sob of relief as he kissed the length of a scar that ran from my belly button down.

I was trembling, and he reached up for my hands before pushing up to his full height and kissing me softly. "Just let me love you, Nat," he murmured, lowering me onto the bed. He followed, tugging his shirt over his head and tossing it somewhere, before reaching for my legs. He kissed all the way down my right leg as he removed my leggings, then all the way back up and over my hip. "Please?"

He was holding out a hand. I took it, letting him lead me to sit astride him. He was still dressed from the waist down, his jeans rough between my legs, and I raised up slightly to avoid the feel of them rubbing. His hands had found my breasts as I dipped my head to kiss him, looping my arms around his neck. "I think I can do that."

## CHAPTER NINE

Waking up in his arms for the second time in as many days felt incredible. It felt right. He was right. As I pulled myself out of the fog of sleep, I felt optimistic and happy. We could make it work. The distance thing wouldn't be too difficult, we both had jobs. We both had lives that were separate from each other. If anything, the distance would stop us from making too many mistakes.

I kissed his cheek and shuffled out of bed, reaching for my shirt and shrugging it on before he woke up. He'd seen it all the night before, but that didn't mean I was happy to bare my body again. I didn't want to have to discuss it on an empty stomach before work.

"I didn't expect you to run out on me the second time around."

I shook my head and smiled, fastening the last of the buttons. "I'm not running. I'm making sure you don't make me late for work again."

He pulled me back, laying me on the bed, and lowered his face over mine. He was upside down and grinning. "I could get you a day off."

"Don't even joke about it. No. I have to get to work," I said, struggling to sit up.

He held my shoulders and kissed me before letting me up. I was slipping on my leggings when he said, "I have to go back down to

Cambridge today. The soonest I can get back up for the weekend is in two weeks."

I wasn't sure how to respond to that. Part of me wanted to suggest he stay one more night, but the rest of me needed some time to get my head around everything. The distance was good. Judging by what he'd said the night before, he wasn't planning to leave and never come back. That meant I had to get used to him calling, messaging, and arranging visits. I hadn't had anything like that for years. I wasn't sure how to handle a relationship of any kind after my marriage had ended so horribly. "But you'll call?"

"Every day. I'll book back in here for the weekend before I leave. I'll be here by the time you get off work."

I nodded, getting up from the bed. "Can we leave early? I don't want anyone seeing you drop me off at the office, and I need to run home to get changed."

He cupped the back of his neck with his hand and looked at me for a moment, studying my face. "Yeah. No problem. Give me five minutes to get changed, and we'll go. Okay?"

I nodded and smiled, watching him get out of bed, feeling my pulse race at the sight of the erection he was sporting.

"You're sure you don't want to stay longer?" he asked with a cheeky wink.

I shook my head, swallowing. "No."

"Not sure?"

"No. So get dressed."

He chuckled as he went into the bathroom, and I finished getting dressed, feeling happier than I had in years.

* * *

He pulled out of my street slowly. My neighbors were never very good at conscientious parking and it was like a slalom getting out of here. I smirked at him as he cursed under his breath, trying not to scratch his ridiculous car. I was not looking forward to the questions coming my way when my neighbors got a chance to speak to me.

"I wanted to ask you something," he said when we were on the main road through town. It was busy with commuter traffic, but he seemed happy to crawl along and talk to me. The change in his manner didn't escape me, it was the same as when we were having coffee and he dropped all his awkwardness and became all business like.

"Yeah?"

"We've had sex three times, Nat, and it's—"

"I won't be getting pregnant if that's what you're worried about. I'm very well protected," I snapped. I probably shouldn't have, but I was shocked at the casual way he approached the subject of us being intimate, and it was a reflex. Softening my tone, I added, "I do appreciate you using condoms though. Safety and all that."

"That wasn't what I was going to ask you," he said as soon as I stopped talking. "I wondered if there was a reason you didn't orgasm. I assumed nerves, but…"

I looked away, staring at the road ahead. Of all the things to be asked, this was never something I would have expected. Mostly because no one had ever given a shit before, but also because it wasn't something I thought about. Ever. "What sort of a question is that?"

"A serious one. If I'm doing something wrong, I want to know about it and fix it."

I hadn't been expecting that. Shame colored my cheeks as I muttered, "It doesn't matter."

He pulled into the car park outside the office, and I ground my teeth. I wanted to get out of the car, to avoid the rest of the conversation, but I couldn't bring myself to open the door. Once I stepped out, that was it for two weeks. The way the conversation was going this could be it, full stop.

He turned in his seat to look directly at me and reached for my hand. "Of course, it matters. There's no point if you don't get off. I want you to… Well, I want you to get the same things I do from this. That means fully enjoying each other's company in and out of bed. When did you last have one? I remember the last you had with me, and that was a very long time ago."

I didn't know what to say. I looked at him and lifted my chin, about to snap an answer when he gave me a meaningful look and added, "During sex."

I shrugged and looked away, cheeks still aflame.

"I can wait. I know you know how long it's been."

"A couple of months after I got married," I said quietly. "Around eleven years ago."

His eyes hardened, but he didn't say anything.

"What? Expected it to have been more recent? We didn't all go on to have perfect lives after you took off, Jason. The rest of us were dealt some shitty cards."

"What does that mean?"

"Nothing. I should go." I reached for the door handle.

"No, you shouldn't. You should stay where you are and talk to me."

I swallowed, trying to get rid of the lump forming in my throat, and shook my head. "I can't. Please, Jase."

"You can, Nat. If we're going to stand a chance we must communicate. Running didn't get us anywhere before."

That was rich. "You were the one running."

He dropped my hand and turned to face the steering wheel, gripping it with both hands. "I shouldn't have. It was the biggest mistake I ever made, Nat, believe me. I've paid for it. Fuck, you've paid for it. But I can't make up for it if you won't talk to me."

Tears welled in my eyes. "You can't make up for it. We can't just go back, we've both changed too much. But this, you thinking you know... I can't."

"What happened to you?" I could hear the pain in his voice. The desperation of needing to know, of wanting to make things right, but not being equipped.

I wasn't sure he could. Nothing could make it right. I was kidding myself. I couldn't have a normal relationship any more than I could relax enough to have a fucking orgasm. Not with him or anyone else. I'd tried and failed before.

"Why can't you let me in?"

"Because…" I was close to saying it, but I diverted at the last second, "I'm damaged. You don't need it. You don't need me. You have everything, Jase. I'm not—"

"Don't." He turned to face me again. "Do not say that."

I squeezed my eyes shut. It was true. It always had been. It was why he ran off without a word. It was why everything I touched had fallen apart. I wasn't good enough. "It always turns to shit, Jase. Believe me, I've watched it happen over and over. I'm not good for you."

He didn't stop me from leaving. I got out of his car and walked to the office with my bottom lip clamped between my teeth. It wasn't until I reached the entrance to the building that his car door slammed, and he ran after me.

I stood perfectly still as he stopped behind me, a little out of breath.

"Talk to me."

I shook my head. I could feel the warmth of his body behind mine, and I was desperate to turn and bury my face in his chest. For him to hold me and for me to feel safe.

"Please. Don't walk away. Come back, let's… Nat, all I want to do is make things right."

I closed my eyes and let the tears fall. If I went back, I had to give him something. I wasn't sure he wanted to hear the truth. I certainly didn't want to go through telling him. But I didn't want to walk away from him. Not really. The last couple of days had been the happiest I'd been in years. Because of him. I was able to be myself and not fear the person I was spending my time with. He made me happy.

"I don't want to talk. Not yet. I will tell you why I'm like this, but I need to think about it."

I had a choice. Stay or go. Staying meant talking. I wasn't ready.

He stepped forward, his chest pressing against my back, and his breath was hot on the shell of my ear. "Whatever you need," he whispered. "Anything, just don't push me away. I can't… I want this. I want you. I want it to work this time."

I looked at our distorted reflection in the blackout glass door and brushed away my tears. "Me too. But I need to go."

He sighed, and kissed my cheek. Apparently, that gesture was his acceptance. I reached out and pushed open the door, stepping away from him.

My phone was going off before I reached my desk. There was no one around, but I could hear Tony in his office. I went straight to the kitchen to make coffee for myself and Tony. I opened the message as I waited for the kettle to boil.

*I just want you to be happy.*

I typed out a reply but didn't send it until I was at my desk.

*I'm trying to be. I'll call you tomorrow. I promise.*

## CHAPTER TEN

*I* needed to let off some steam. That meant a work out. Haylie met me at the gym once I promised her news on the whole Jase development, and we started the session with her glaring at me, expecting instant gratification. I didn't oblige until we stopped for a rest.

"You fucked him, didn't you?"

"Nice. Yes, I slept with him."

"His place or yours?"

"His hotel. Sunday and last night. Twice last night…"

Despite being a sweating, panting mess, she was grinning at me.

"What?"

"When are you seeing him again?"

"A week from Friday. He can't get back up before then, he runs the Cambridge office and is back and forth a lot."

"He what?"

I pressed my lips together, trying to hide the smile. It was ridiculous however I said it, and I knew how she was about to react. "Apparently, the L on the company name stands for Locksley…"

She started cackling, drawing the attention of a few of the other women in the group. I lowered my voice to a harsh whisper. "Will you shush?"

"He's your fucking boss, and you didn't know? Oh, this is fucking priceless. Didn't you check?"

"All right, calm down," I muttered, putting my water bottle down and picking up my bell. "No, I didn't. He left this area years ago, I didn't think he'd be back, not after his mum moved south. Anyway, the individual names aren't listed anywhere, everything comes addressed to So and So at LGW Solutions. I'd have worked it out eventually, but to be honest, my head's been up my arse since he turned up a few weeks ago."

She was still chuckling and shaking her head. "Only you, Nat. So, you're an item now?"

I frowned. "I wouldn't go that far…"

She knew what that meant. "What happened?"

I swallowed hard. "We had words this morning before he left. He said something, I snapped—well you know how I react sometimes—and walked away. I said I'd call him tomorrow. After a day to think on it, I'm not sure I can be bothered with the stress to be honest."

"Words about…" Her eyes widened as she waited for me to elaborate.

I rolled my eyes and glanced around before mouthing sex.

"Oh, god. What happened? Did you fart? I mean, it happens. I let out a massive fanny fart once. Nearly died laughing."

I glared at her in mute horror for a second before I managed to hiss, "What's fucking wrong with you? No! He wanted me to explain something I wasn't comfortable discussing. Not yet, I hardly know him."

Folding her arms over her chest, she glowered at me. "Well, that's a load of shit, you've known him all your life."

"It's like talking to the wall," I said, turning back to the class instructor as she clapped her hands to indicate it was time to continue with the session. "I need time. He moves too fast. We sorted it before he left though. I think…"

She sighed. "Well you'll find out a week from Friday, won't you?"

"I said I'd call tomorrow," I said quietly as the class resumed.

* * *

I sat in the car, radio playing, looking at my phone. It felt like days since I had last spoken to him, not a few hours. There was no logic to it. We weren't a couple. I shouldn't miss him, not after just two nights together. Certainly not after the conversation we had that morning. I'd been so embarrassed. I didn't know men could tell if women faked it. I didn't think they gave a shit. I assumed they were just in it to get theirs and go to sleep. If nothing else, I'd learned something.

Jason was different.

I should have known he meant it. He really wanted to make me happy. He cared how I felt. It was how he'd always been, right up until he left. One thing I didn't expect was for him to accept the scars that marred my body. I expected questions and revulsion, not tender kisses and reassurances.

There wasn't much daylight left, and I looked through the windscreen at my house. Almost everything of consequence that had happened in my life after Jason, had taken place in this house. My whole adult life was contained in these four walls. I'd hated it for a long time, but not as much as I did in this moment. I didn't want to go inside. I didn't want to return to a life that brought me so much misery. It hadn't been the easiest two days, but faced with my empty house and the ghosts that followed me around it, I knew which I preferred. But he wasn't here. He couldn't be. We lived different lives. I worked, paid my bills, and spent time with my only real friend when we had time. He ran a multi-million-pound company, lived in Cambridge near his mum, and probably spent time with his family. His life was hours away and didn't include me. It couldn't.

Grabbing my water bottle, I opened the car door and stepped out onto the drive. The same familiar shiver ran down my spine, and I steeled myself against the flood of memories. Anyone else would have moved. Anyone else would have walked away from that house. But I'd never been one for running away. I used the feelings the memories invoked as a shield. I spent seven years drawing strength from everything I'd lived through, but it wasn't working. Not tonight.

I was almost at the door when my phone rang.

I answered and stuck my key in the lock. "Hello?"

"I know you said tomorrow, but I needed to know you were okay."

The relief was instant. I didn't care if he heard the breath I exhaled. "I am now."

There was a moment's silence. I stood on my front step with the key still in the lock, waiting for his response.

"Good. I mean, I was worried. I didn't want you to… Well, I wasn't sure if I'd offended you and…"

I smiled at his rambling and pushed open the door. "It's fine, Jase. Thank you for checking in though."

I went straight into the kitchen and looked at the fridge, then turned around and went straight upstairs as he said, "Am I intruding?"

"No," I replied quickly, going into my room and sitting on the edge of my bed. "I just got in from a workout, and I'm shattered. I assume you got home okay?"

"Yeah, the roads were quiet. One of the teams was called out to a leak in Norfolk. I swung by to help, so I just got back myself."

"That was quick," I said, wiggling out of my gym clothes and putting them in the laundry basket inside my wardrobe. Then I stood in front of the mirror on the door and looked at myself. At the squishy parts of my body I hadn't managed to tone up. At the scars that weren't covered by my underwear, wondering how he'd kept from recoiling from them. I traced them with my eyes but didn't touch them. I hated how they felt as much as I hated how they looked. Raised blemishes that felt smooth to the touch, but I couldn't feel anything around them because the nerves there were damaged, which explains why I hadn't realized he'd felt them. Each one was a constant reminder, an imprint of a part of my life I would be reminded of every time I looked at myself.

He laughed, pulling my attention away from my body and back to him. "A rival company had it first, turned out they couldn't handle it. They'd already dug it out and had the water turned off. I called and had them turn the water on as soon as I got there, fitted the rig and left the guys to clean it up."

I turned off the light and climbed into bed. "What time will they get home?"

"They won't, I sorted them rooms for the night. Any other work questions or can we get back to talking about you?"

My stomach turned over at the notion being important enough to be the sole topic of conversation. "I don't like talking about me."

"Humor me," he said seriously. "What are you wearing?" He changed to a playful, cheeky tone.

I choked. "What?"

He was silent. Waiting. I couldn't even hear him breathing.

I pressed my lips together and closed my eyes. "Just underwear. I'm in bed."

"I'd rather be there with you."

A flutter of excitement turned in my stomach. "Where are you?"

"Sitting in my car in the garage in the dark, thinking about you in your underwear."

"That's…"

"Yeah, sounds creepy when you say it out loud. But it's true. Well, the underwear part is a new development since you brought it up. I'm not that big a pervert, but you mentioned it and my mind does stuff."

I set off laughing. "I miss you." It was out before I could stop it. I didn't mean to say it out loud.

"If I could be back up there sooner, I would be. Really. I have stuff I'm needed for here, otherwise I'd be on the road."

I believed it. I wanted it. But he had responsibilities like I did. Bigger. I almost offered to go to him but lost my nerve at the last second. "It'll fly," I said instead. "We can always call each other, can't we?"

"What sort of workout do you do?" he asked, changing the subject.

Confused by his sudden change in direction, I answered, "Just kettlebells. I need it for core strength after… after the accident. It's kept me right for years. Haylie isn't a fan, but she comes with me when she can."

"But she goes with you even though she doesn't like it?"

"Yep. She came with me when I first started for moral support. It ended up being a sort of habit. She does that with me, I do karaoke with her." Talking about her made me feel so grateful for her friendship. I smiled to myself.

"Sounds like a fair trade off to me. So, you still sing?"

"I drink too much and shout down a mic. Yeah," I teased. I'd forgotten he used to listen to me sing. I often won the karaoke contest in our local pub and kept us in free jugs of beer on Thursday nights.

"I'll have to remember that. Nat, sorry, I have to go," he said abruptly. "Can I call you tomorrow?"

I frowned. "I thought I was calling you?"

"What time will you be home?" he asked. He suddenly seemed in a rush to end the call.

"From six. Is everything okay?"

"Yeah, yeah, it's fine. I'm just tired. It's been a long day. I'll call tomorrow."

"Okay. Erm… Goodnight."

"I'll be thinking about you."

The call ended before I could respond, and I dropped the phone on the bed at my side and flopped back on my pillow. I was probably reading too much into it, but his hot then cold manner had me wondering what was wrong with him. He called me, he wanted to speak to me, then he couldn't wait to get off the phone. He hadn't behaved that way the last two days. It was weird.

Could someone have interrupted him? I pushed the thought away. That assumption wouldn't lead anywhere positive, and he'd told me he was single. I had no reason to think he'd lied to me. He was probably just tired. I knew I was, and I hadn't been crawling around in a hole all evening. It had been a long twelve hours, and he'd had the same start to the day I had.

I turned on my side and opened my phone. Before I lost my nerve, I sent a message.

*Thanks for checking in. I know I said I'd contact you tomorrow, but I think I really needed it.*

I watched three little dots bounce at the bottom of my screen and felt a flutter in my stomach.

*I'm thinking about you ;)*

I fell asleep feeling positive. I had a job that was perfect for me. I had the best friend anyone could ever ask for. Jason was back in my life, and for the time being, it wasn't terrible. The ghosts of my past that usually tormented me were quiet tonight, and I hoped they'd stay quiet after. It was silly, but I was sure Jase had chased them away.

## CHAPTER ELEVEN

The light was on.

"Trust me."

It was barely a whisper as his tongue circled my right nipple. I wanted to. God, I wanted to with as badly as I wanted him. It had been the longest ten days of my life, waiting for him to come back, but he didn't know what he was asking of me.

His hand was stroking my inner thigh. With each down stroke, he came closer and closer to the apex of my thighs, and I wiggled my hips in encouragement.

His lips were beside my belly button, and he smiled against my skin. "Not yet."

It was the worst kind of torture. I wanted to scream in frustration. I might not have reached an orgasm, but it didn't mean I couldn't love the feel of him inside me, and that's what I wanted. "Ja… Jase." I couldn't speak. I was nervous and excited all at once, my stomach churning in anticipation of what he was planning to do. Longing to feel more of him.

"Trust me."

His mouth moved lower. His breath was hot on my inner thigh

where his hand had been moments before, then his lips brushed the sensitive skin.

"It'll be worth it."

He sucked. At first it was painful, but it changed instantly, the sensation triggering a response elsewhere. My abdominal muscles clenched, and I pushed my hips down into the mattress. He followed, closing his mouth over my clit and rolling his tongue over the exposed nub.

It felt wrong. No. Not wrong. It felt good. Just, unfamiliar. I wanted to roll away from him. To make the sensations stop. But he wasn't going to let me. Not unless I specifically told him no. If I said that one word he'd back off. He'd promised. But he had specifically said he wanted to watch me come before he got his.

I didn't know what to do with my hands, so I grasped his hair. All that did was push his face further into me. His response was to suck harder on my clit.

A wave of coldness ran through my body from my feet up. "Please." In my head, I screamed it. The reality was I'd just about managed a whisper. "Oh…"

Two fingers slid inside me, moving in time with his mouth. He was going to tease an orgasm from me if it killed him. I could feel it building, and I didn't know what to do about it.

Hot and cold. I could feel the two sensations racing through my veins, vying for control of me as Jason inched me closer and closer. My hips were moving, my fingers tangled in his hair, and I could feel the orgasm he'd been determined to give me surging to the surface. I was right there, on the edge of a precipice, and he felt it. He felt me clench around his fingers, my mind warring with the need to let it go and the need to suppress it.

Keeping his fingers inside me, stroking my g-spot, he moved up the bed and kissed me. I could taste myself on him, the salty tang of my arousal, and that undid me. I clung to him as the force wracked my body. It ran through me in waves, the epicenter clutching at his fingers still inside me and moving out through my extremities.

It hadn't stopped when he pulled away from me and moved down my body again.

"Oh, god... Please..."

He ignored my panted plea and ran his tongue over my clit again. My body jerked, and he withdrew his fingers, looked up at me, and grinned. "Go with it."

He drew a second from me without much effort, using his mouth to massage my clit with expert skill. It tingled on my skin for what felt like minutes as the waves of pleasure ebbed away.

I was panting when he lowered himself over me, settling between my legs. He stroked a hand over my hair and kissed me as he slid inside. I froze.

"Did you..."

"Yes." He smiled before kissing me. Then he began to move. Each grind of his hips was slow, controlled, and he watched me. "Are you okay?"

I let out a small laugh and smiled, running my hands over his shoulders and up the sides of his neck. He shivered at my touch and groaned, bending his head to kiss me. His thrusts became longer. Deeper. They felt amazing after my two orgasms, he filled me, satisfied me, felt right inside me. Then he picked up pace. With his head bowed, breathing heavily in my ear, he came to his own orgasm quickly.

"Fuck..."

His orgasm wracked his body. I held him for a few moments, stroking the back of his head before he rolled off and removed the condom. "Sorry."

I turned my head to the side. "What? Why?"

"I didn't think... Well, it's been a couple of weeks... Are you okay?"

I grinned. "Perfect."

It was true. I hadn't been this vulnerable with anyone in so long, and I wasn't sure I would be able to relax. I was so nervous. He'd told me he'd wait all night if he had to, and he wasn't getting off until I had. The fear of disappointing him was crippling.

I had missed him terribly, though. Every phone call had built the anticipation. Every conversation had been a step closer to being with him again, and the promise of having him, of feeling like myself again, had overridden the nerves.

He rolled onto his side and looked into my eyes. "You're so beautiful, Nathalie. I can't believe I found you again."

I lowered my eyes and felt my cheeks flush.

"What's wrong?" he asked, catching my gaze.

"I'm not. I mean, I don't feel…"

He moved so quickly I couldn't stop him from parting my legs and kneeling between them. I lay there and looked up at him, watching him as he studied my body.

"Jase…" I said, reaching for the blanket to cover myself.

"Stop. I think you're beautiful." He reached out a hand and ran a finger over some of my scars. "These don't affect that. I don't care about them. They aren't what I love about you."

I blinked up at him. He carried on, "You're beautiful in every way a person can be. I don't know what exactly you've been through, but you came out on the other side, and you're still the same woman I loved all those years ago."

I licked my suddenly parched lips.

"Say something."

I shook my head.

"Are you going to tell me how you got them?"

I closed my eyes and sighed, then shuffled up the bed, teasing the duvet down. I arranged it so I was fully covered, hiding beneath it, before meeting his gaze.

"I was run over." My voice shook.

He moved closer, reaching for my hand. I let him take it, and he rubbed his thumb over my palm as he waited for me to find the words.

I decided on the spot to tell him. If I concentrated too much I'd lock up, and he needed to know. He wouldn't keep pressing if it weren't important to him. It wasn't how I wanted to tell him, but for the first time I was able to. He'd seen the mess. He deserved to know what caused it.

"I got in from work late…" I paused, wondering if I was making a mistake. He squeezed my hand reassurance, so I carried on, "I knew better, but I got talking to an old friend from school. She asked how I was, I told her I was married. Asked who to." I smiled sadly. "Her face was a picture when I said his name. He'd been shagging her for months. Obviously, I was furious. I walked through the door, and he grabbed me as soon as it was closed, which was normal if I was late. He grabbed my hair and pulled my head back. Demanded to know who I was fucking. My answer was 'well it's not Michaela Jones.'"

His brows raised as he recognised the name, but he didn't say anything.

I took a breath. "He punched me in the face. My nose broke immediately. He usually kept it to where it wouldn't be seen, but I think I shocked him. I started screaming at him. He lost his temper, probably more shocked that I was defending myself, and really went for it. I managed to get out of the house, no idea how, but he caught up with me in the drive. Another slap, I fell, and he jumped into his Defender. I must have hit my head, because I didn't get out of the way. The pain must have made me black out again. But…" I paused and ran my free hand over my abdomen. "The neighbors heard, phoned the police and an ambulance. I landed in the worst possible position, they said. Three tons of Land Rover crushed my pelvis. It took twenty-four hours and two surgeries to get the internal bleeding under control. Another one to pin my pelvis and femur."

My throat was dry. He hadn't moved an inch while I'd told him the whole story, his hand still holding mine. His face was expressionless. Not knowing if that was good or bad I swallowed, took a steadying breath, and kept talking while I still could.

"They got me on my feet then sent me home. I carried on with therapy and was good to go back to work two years later. I made it to the hearing, dragged myself into court on crutches. He was sentenced to seven years. That was a reduced sentence with conditions. He gave me the divorce I demanded, signed over the house I paid for anyway, and agreed to adhere to a lifetime restraining order. It wasn't enough, but it was all the justice I was going to get. So I sorted myself out, got back to work, and here I am." I tried to smile, but that was a step too far, so I chewed my bottom lip and waited for him to respond.

"What is his name?" he asked eventually.

I hadn't said it for years. I tried not to even think it. I changed my name by deed poll the day my divorce was finalized. I didn't want to see, hear, or speak it again. "Gav H-Holt," I whispered, lowering my head. I didn't need to see his face to know what his reaction was going to be. We all knew Gav. We were all wary of him when we were younger. He was never good news. He was always up to something unpleasant.

Jason was off the bed and tugging on his boxers as he said, "Fuck… I hurt you so badly you thought he was all you were worth?"

I didn't have a reply. That wasn't how I saw it, but I supposed he had a point.

"I made you feel so worthless you thought that bastard… He was always fucked up."

"I put up with shit I shouldn't have. I didn't help my—"

He was pacing. "If I hadn't fucking left you, he wouldn't have gotten near you."

I couldn't stop the incredulous laugh from escaping. "What?"

"It's my fault."

I was caught between misery and fury. I was also stuck hiding my unsightly body beneath the comforter, so my options for a response were limited to verbal. I clenched my jaw in frustration, not sure what to say, and between clenched teeth I managed to murmur, "It isn't about you."

He finally paused to look at me while tears streamed down my face. I don't know if it was my tears or my words that made him stop.

"I… no. No. I'm sorry." I watched him deflate. The rage in his eyes gave way to sadness. The anger he'd been feeling was swept away by apology and regret.

I held out my hand. "Just… Please. I didn't tell you so that you'd get angry. I told you because you deserved to know the truth about me. Why I'm so… like this."

"You're perfect."

Usually, I'd have brushed off something like this with a laugh and a joke, but I couldn't. He meant it, I could see it in his eyes and hear it in the tremor of his voice. I blinked back more tears as he crawled over the bed to me. He didn't take his eyes from mine as he took my face in his hands and kissed me.

"I love everything about you. Everything. To think what he did to you…"

That was twice he'd used that word tonight. Three times total, if I recalled correctly. I hadn't felt loved in years. Not by anyone but Haylie, but she didn't count. The need to make him feel better was overwhelming, to take away whatever pain he was feeling, to show him I loved things about him, too. But all I could manage was, "It doesn't matter, Jase. It happened. It's done. It was another life."

"A life you shouldn't have had to live." He kissed me again and rested his forehead against mine. "I have so much to make up for."

The tone of his voice, the regret, pierced my chest. He was blaming the decision he made for what that monster had done to me, and I couldn't stand it. I cleared my throat and pressed my hand against his chest, pushing him back a few inches. "We can't change what happened. We make choices, I made choices. We do whatever feels right at the time, and we live with the consequences. You left and built a life. I'm sure you've had stuff to deal with. I made a bad choice. I kept making bad choices for years until they nearly killed me. We can't keep looking back. It isn't good for us. We've got to keep trying to make it better. I'm here with you. We're, well, whatever this is, we're here making it together. It's new. And it's good. Don't let him spoil it, Jase. Please."

A few seconds passed. He didn't look away as he worked through whatever thoughts were in his head. He remained there, my hand still on his chest, looking into my eyes.

"Look," I said, starting to feel uncomfortable. "At first I didn't want to do this. I didn't want to see you. I didn't want to revisit the past. But you showed me this is different. We aren't the same people. We're older and wiser, and we won't make the same mistakes. All that we've lived through brought us here."

"Is this where you want to be?" he asked quietly, moving back.

My hand lost contact with his chest. I let it fall into my lap, and he watched me, waiting for my response. I thought about it carefully. He was asking for a declaration, and I had to be certain. He'd subtly made his.

"More than anything."

The tension left his body. His shoulders relaxed, his features softened, and he smiled. "Okay."

"Okay?"

He turned off the light, and pulled me into his arms. I gladly went, resting my head on his bare shoulder as his free arm circled my waist, fingers brushing up and down my back. He kissed the top of my head and whispered, "Yeah. Everything's okay."

## CHAPTER TWELVE

He left the bed and I tried not to tug the sheets up to cover myself as he went into the bathroom. We're past that. At least, I was trying to get past it.

When he came back, I gave him an awkward smile.

"What's up?" he asked, walking around to his side the bed.

"I need more practice at this."

He leaned over me, a hand on either side of my head, and kissed me. "Why?"

I grimaced. "My dismount isn't as graceful as it could be with a condom to think about."

He barked a laugh he lay at my side. "I was wondering… You said you were covered," he said thoughtfully. "Covered well?"

I pulled my brows in and looked at him. "Incredibly well covered. Why?"

"Well, I've always been very careful, we could…" He frowned and shook his head. "No. Forget it."

I chewed my lip. I wasn't expecting this conversation, but it was worth having. "I'm clean. I got checked out after… And there was only one after and he used… I mean…" I said awkwardly. "There's only you, and I can guarantee no babies and no nasty surprises here."

"Guarantee is a strong word, but the usual ninety nine percent suits me," he replied with a soft laugh. He was quiet for a second, then added, "I'm clean. I'm only seeing you. It's your decision, but I trust you and it removes that particular... discomfort. I just want you to be comfortable. Confident."

I smiled as he pulled the duvet back over me.

"And confidence takes time," he said, kissing my forehead. "I enjoyed that."

I smiled and pressed my face into his chest.

"Hey..." he said quietly.

I looked up. He was grinning, I decided to probe, "How did you get so good at... Well, you have a talent."

He sighed, and I noticed a subtle shift in his demeanor. "You really want to know?" he asked, looking serious.

I asked myself if I did, and instantly decided it couldn't be any worse than the horror story I'd told him. I nodded.

"Okay," he said with a resigned sigh. "When my marriage broke down, and we separated, I wasn't ready for a relationship, but was ready for female company."

I was interested and shuffled away so I could prop up on my elbows to listen.

"So, I joined a club. I didn't just go there to fuck anything that moved. I..." He pressed his lips together and thought for a moment. "I had a drink and a few conversations and found someone I clicked with."

"You joined a sex club?" I couldn't keep the surprise out of my voice. Not because it was a shocking thing to hear, I'd just never spoken to anyone who'd done that before.

He shrugged, apparently comfortable with my reaction. "Yeah. Met a woman, hit it off with her, and we met a couple of times a month at the club. I met her needs, she met mine. No drama. No emotional attachment. No expectations."

He spoke about it so casually. Was I odd for finding it unusual? "So... Like kinky sex dungeon fuck buddies?"

He shook his head and raised his arm, inviting me to cuddle into him. I stayed where I was, and he frowned, but continued his explanation. "No. Nothing like that. Safety was paramount. Her needs were very specific, and I respected her boundaries. No marking of the skin, only gentle touch, which was perfect for me because I don't get my kicks that way. No unprotected contact including oral, which again was perfect for me. She needed to feel safe and respected, which I hope I managed, she didn't say anything to the contrary. All the club did was provide a private, neutral location."

I had questions, too many questions, and I didn't know how to ask them. He was looking at me, waiting for me to say something. When I didn't, he went on, "She has her own very successful business, no time to commit to a new relationship, and doesn't particularly want one. We helped each other out."

"When did you last see her?"

"A few days before I first saw you in the bar," he said confidently. "I cancelled our next meeting because I couldn't get you out of my head, and haven't seen her since. I decided to call it off completely when you agreed to meet me for coffee."

My brows rose. "You were that confident?"

"Hopeful."

"And she was okay with you just… dumping her?"

"It was a formal arrangement, not a relationship. Business really. I saw her because I wasn't ready for a relationship but had needs, and I stopped seeing her when I found someone I wanted a relationship with."

And that answered my next question, how he was able to just discuss the matter so calmly? It explained how he made the switch from uncertain Jase to confident Jason, able to discuss matters calmly. It was business. "So, she didn't mean anything to you?"

He smiled at me. "Not in a romantic sense, no. I respect her, she's a great person. She works very hard to provide for her family, supports her community, and took great care of herself to make sure she could do that. Those few hours a month were how she let off steam. Like I did."

"I thought those places were," I hesitated, trying to find the right word, "seedy?"

He shook his head, his eyes shining with amusement. "There are different rooms for different... things," he said with a quiet chuckle. "All needs can be met, but mine and hers, were simpler."

"And what are they?"

"I," he said, moving over me, "get my kicks from seeing you getting yours."

I didn't fully understand. "I thought it was all whips and chains? You know, leather and kink?"

He kissed me, catching my bottom lip between his and sucking it gently. "That's a very broad term. We all have a kink."

"I don't..."

"No?" he asked, kissing along my jaw. "Maybe you just haven't found it yet."

I snorted. "Right."

"I'm serious. You won't be into pain, obviously, and honestly I don't like causing it, even to meet that end, but there's nothing to say you don't get off on," he looked at me for a second, as though thinking hard, "sensory."

"Which is?"

He resumed kissing my neck, licking along the pulse point and blowing on the slick trail of saliva he left there. It chilled, and I shivered. He moved further down, toward my breasts. "Hot. Cold. Light. Dark. Silence. Sound. Gentle restraint to stop you from wriggling away while I tease you with tickles and prickles and... other things."

I remembered how he used to lie with me in the cornfield behind my house, watching the bats come out at sunset. He'd always have one arm under my head, the other tickling up and down my arm or back. The times that had turned into something far more were too many to count. I wondered if he remembered also.

The awkward fumbling hadn't gone on long when we'd started sleeping together. I didn't discuss it with my friends back then, but experience had taught me that Jason had been a very considerate partner. He didn't race to the finish line. I remembered a number of times when he didn't bother at all, content to give me the attention. And I didn't orgasm. It took over a year of us being sexually active for me to experience that particular joy. And a few short weeks after that, he was gone.

"But only if you want to," he added, his lips leaving my body. I opened my eyes to find he'd moved back up the bed and was looking down at my face.

"I…" I licked my lips, then swallowed. "I don't know… You can't get me all worked up then fire questions at me like that."

"Okay. What if I go and buy you some *gifts,* and we can have some fun trying them out?"

I chewed my lip. I was up for it. I was happy to try new things, I just hadn't had such a candid conversation before. "Okay…"

His hand grasped mine and he pulled me from the bed.

"What…"

"Shower."

"Together?" I sounded really stupid, I know, and his laugh confirmed it. "I…"

He led me into the bathroom by the hand, turning on the shower and holding me in front of the mirror. I watched as he pulled my hair over one shoulder, kissing the one he exposed. His skin was darker than mine, not too tanned, but enough to notice I spent very little time outside despite summer only just passing. I wasn't sure if it was from working outdoors or lots of holidays. It didn't look like a sunbed tan, and it certainly wasn't sprayed on. His hair was lighter than mine, his shoulders easily as broad as mine, and he stood six inches taller than me. My breasts weren't the perky ones he'd enjoyed when we were younger. I was a good three dress sizes bigger. My hips were broad, and my waist wasn't that well defined. A lump formed in my throat as I looked at myself, but he didn't appear to see what I did, judging by the erection pressed against my ass.

"Together. I want to do everything together with you."

"Together, together?"

His arms circled my waist. "Yeah. You and me. Us," he said in my ear.

"That's what you want?"

"That's all I want."

I turned and met his gaze. "I... You're sure?"

"I've never been more sure of anything in my life."

I kissed him. My hands found his face and held him to me for a few moments before I grabbed hold of his hair.

"Is that a yes?" he asked against my lips.

"Yes, it's a yes," I confirm, backing him into the shower.

The water hit his body and sprayed onto mine. It was cold, and my body responded accordingly. He laughed against my lips as I pressed into him with a sharp intake of breath, and he reached for my breasts. Erect, my nipples were sensitive, and my breath hitched as his rough palms ran over them.

"You like that?"

I made an appreciative sound low in my throat as he dipped his head and kissed the sensitive spot beneath my ear.

"And..."

Pinching nipples between the finger and thumb of each hand, he sucked my earlobe into his mouth. I responded by tipping my head back, arching my spine, and pressing my body against his.

He moved on, sliding his hands down my sides to my hips, then turned me around so I was under the falling water. I could feel his erection on the bare skin of my ass again. I knew he wasn't wearing protection. I didn't care. He told me it was okay, and I believed him. I wanted to feel him inside me, nothing at all separating us. I wanted it to be how it used to be, before the heartbreak and the loathing, how it was when all I knew was being loved by him.

I backed up.

"Wait..." he murmured into my ear, brushing his hands over my hips.

He was going to stop. "No. Please, Jase. I don't..."

His groan told me all I needed to know. It carried in the tiled bathroom, above the sound of the shower, rivalled only by my gasp as he thrust deep. Every muscle contracted around him, and I almost cried out as he completely withdrew. His voice in my ear stopped me.

"This is... god, you're everything."

He thrust back inside, and for the first time in too many years, I felt everything he said he wanted me to feel. I was perfect. I was complete. I was where I was supposed to be.

The water beat down on my back, interrupted occasionally by his body as he kissed me, or his arm as he reached for my shoulder, but the sensation of the hot water, combined with the feel of him deep inside me, set off a reaction deep in my core. It began as a contraction, my internal muscles clenching around his cock, and traveled outward in a series of chills. I recognised it and bent over, pushing my ass back, urging him deeper. Steadying myself against the cold, tiled wall with one hand, I reached back for him with the other, splaying my hand on his abdomen.

The chills that traversed my body, spreading through my extremities, were followed by another sensation. Heat. Pouring through my veins, the orgasm tore through me, and I couldn't stop myself from crying out his name. That undid him. He reached for me, grasping both breasts and pulling me against his chest as he came. I felt every twitch inside of me, every ragged breath against my neck as he came down from his own high.

From nowhere, laughter bubbled in my chest. Beginning as a quiet chuckle as it grew to a full, joyful laugh.

"Why are you laughing?" he asked as I rested my head on his shoulder.

"I don't know."

He kissed the side of my head and ran his fingers down my sides as he withdrew. "That was something."

"Hmm." I smiled and turned toward him, reaching for his face. He bent and kissed me, then reached for a bottle of body wash on a shelf above my head.

"I think we should go shopping right now," he said, lathering his body.

I watched him wash himself, then squeeze out more soap and begin massaging my shoulders, breasts, and stomach, taking great care to cover every inch of me with bubbles. When he was done, I pursed my lips. "For?"

"If you're going to go off like that, I'll need backup."

I looked away, and he tilted my chin with his finger and kissed me.

"Don't go all shy on me. I've experienced it now, you've set the bar."

He reached for a bottle of shampoo and handed it to me before stepping out. "Take your time. We've got all day."

I watched him wrap a towel around his waist, wondering what the hell I'd agreed to, and took my time washing my hair.

## CHAPTER THIRTEEN

I took them from the bags one at a time. Some of them looked ridiculous, like oversized caricatures of dicks that seemed more like instruments of torture than something designed with pleasure in mind. Jase didn't say anything. I was aware of him in my periphery vision, leaning against the wall, running a thumb over his bottom lip. It was making me feel self-conscious so I looked at him and said, "What?"

"I'm measuring your reactions."

I snorted. "Why?"

"So I know where to start," he answered seriously.

I didn't respond, but studied another box, then opened it and took the small finger sized vibrator from the packaging. "I have one of these."

He ignored my embarrassment. "No point starting there then, is there?" I flicked my eyes his way and heard him huff a quiet laugh. "What about that one?"

I looked at the big purple dildo on the bed and shook my head, checking out another box. "Why the hell have you bought a sports massager?"

His eyes brightened. "There. We start there."

I turned on the bed and looked at him. "With this?"

He nodded his head once. "And a few other things, but yeah."

I put down the bag I was holding a picked up another. "Such as?"

He joined me, taking the bag from me. "You were always big on touch."

I pulled in my brows. "You remember that?"

"I remember everything," he said with a saucy smile followed by a wink.

I gave him my best 'really?' look.

With a flourish, he pulled what looked like an Ostrich feather out of the bag and ran it under my nose. I pulled away, and plucked it from his fingers, laughing. It faded when I saw what was in his hand next. "Okay…"

He turned the small device over, displaying a slowly turning wheel of cruel looking spikes attached to a long silver handle. "Hold out your hand."

I shook my head and inched away. "It'll hurt."

"It won't hurt."

"It's got massive spikes on it!" I hissed, staring at it.

He grasped my hand and held it firmly, then ran the thing up my palm. "Spikes that don't hurt."

I pursed my lips. "All right. So, what do we do, lay this lot out like a big game of Operation or assign each of them a number and roll a dice?"

I watched him put the wheel thing in a small case, drop it on the bed, then reach into the bag again. "Well. I expect you'll fidget quite a bit, so we'll need to use something along these lines," he responded while pointing to the box in his hand.

I frowned. There was a picture of a woman, a slim blonde who looked beautiful in her red lacy lingerie, positioned on a bed with her wrists secured to her thighs. She didn't look distressed, but the thought of being tied down wasn't something that excited me.

"It won't stop you from moving, just keeps you from ruining your own orgasms."

I didn't quite understand. I think my expression said it all.

"It's only Velcro, so it comes right off," he explained. "But we'll leave that alone for now and work up to it, okay?"

He stuffed it back in the bag and dropped it on the floor. I laughed.

He looked at me with a stupid grin. "What?"

"You're going all out on the kinky fuckery, aren't you?"

His snort of laughter made me smile. "This isn't kinky fuckery. This is making it as good as I can get it for you."

"But what's in it for you?" It was a genuine question. I didn't see what he could be getting out of any of this, it was all designed to get me going.

"I get to be the one who gets you there. That's all I want. A happy, fulfilled you. Preferably screaming my name."

I looked back down at the massager and chewed the inside of my bottom lip.

"Tell me what you're thinking."

With everything being brand new, it all needed to be cleaned, charged, and fitted with batteries. It kind of killed any spontaneity the first time.

I had to choose how to go about it. It was my decision to make, he'd made that perfectly clear. After a few moments, I took a deep breath and said, "I'm thinking we better charge this thing."

The grin on his face was ridiculous.

The butterflies that burst into flight in my stomach were worse.

* * *

The rest of the day was spent on a date. A real one.

He drove us out to a strip mall where we had a light lunch of sausage rolls and coffee while sitting in the car. I didn't say it, but I loved every second. Not because I didn't appreciate the dinners in restaurants, but because it was normal. It was something we would have done before, and it just felt like *us*.

We decided on a movie since the cinema was close. Jason chose a spoof thriller, and I'd laughed until I cried. Jase seemed relieved I enjoyed the movie, and when I asked him why, he said, "You seemed nervous going in."

We walked hand in hand across the retail park to his car. Just before we reached the crosswalk, Jase pulled me back and a large Land Rover roared past. I looked up in alarm and flinched back further, sucking in a sharp breath. The smell of the exhaust made my stomach churn, and my limbs locked up.

"Sh… fucking idiot," Jason said, not too quietly, as he looked down at me and squeezed my trembling hand. Eyes searching mine with concern, he asked, "You okay?"

Heart pounding in my chest I held my breath, trying not to get another wave of exhaust fumes, and blinked back tears. "Yeah. Yeah I'm fine."

He pulled me into his chest, wrapping his arms around me protectively. He didn't say anything else, didn't ask any more questions, instead he held me until I'd gotten over the shock.

"I'm okay," I murmured, pulling away. It seemed like such an overreaction, and to have it in front of him was embarrassing. "Shall we just…"

I let him lead me across the street, but just before I got into the car, I looked back. The Land Rover that had almost run me over was parked behind us. It was facing us, and while I could see someone was sitting inside, I couldn't see their face. They weren't getting out, though. They were just sitting there, waiting. Watching.

Feeling even more uneasy, I turned away and moved into the safety of his car.

I didn't mention the vehicle or its occupant, but I was beginning to feel nauseous. I couldn't excuse it all away as being shaken after the near miss on the road.

"What's up?" he questioned, apparently oblivious to the Land Rover.

I shrugged. "Thanks for… well you know."

He leaned in close and murmured, "It's sort of why I'm here," and started his car.

I immediately scanned the car park, looking for the black car, but it wasn't there. I still felt a bit uneasy.

"What shall we do now?" he enquired as he drove through the car park.

I shrugged. "I could always buy you dinner."

"Do I get to choose where we eat?" he asked.

"Yes," I answered, glancing up at him. "Anywhere you like."

"Hmm... all right. No complaining when we get there, though..."

"That's fine," I said, turning on the radio. "My treat."

He drove a couple of miles across the outskirts of the city, pulling into another strip mall and parking outside an Italian chain restaurant.

"You want to eat here?"

"What's wrong with it?"

I shrugged. "Just not your usual choice."

He leaned over, brushing my hair behind my ear and letting his lips graze the lobe. "I'm not trying to impress you, now."

Ignoring the chill that ran over my shoulders, I turned my face to him. "Really?"

"Not with food, anyway."

The way he winked at me was both hilarious and seductive. I wanted to laugh, but there was a seriousness to his tone that hinted at what was to come when we got back to his hotel room.

I wet my lips, and he kissed them. "And I can't do that on an empty stomach."

I shook my head at him and laughed. "Well, we better go in. I don't want you passing out on me."

There was something in the way he looked at me which reminded me of the night of our school leavers party. Like I was the only person in the world he could love. I'd never forgotten it. He looked happy, the same sort of happy I felt when we were together. We sat there for a few moments, just looking at each other, and I realized I could love him. I did love him. I honestly felt it. What surprised me was that it didn't scare me, but I did feel a bit stupid that I hadn't realized it before.

"Jase?"

"Yeah?"

"Can we… go in?"

He kissed me again then got out of the car. I followed, and he walked around his car, taking me by the waist to lead me into the restaurant.

The girl who showed us to our table seemed to really like Jase. I found her fawning uncomfortable, especially when she made a point of touching his shoulder as she placed the oversized menus on the table in front of us. I was getting annoyed, but he didn't seem to notice. He ordered himself a coke while I asked for a glass of wine, and not once did he look away from me while she was at our table.

"Does she know you?" I asked when she set down our drinks and finally moved away.

He frowned, looking at the back of her as she walked to another table. "I don't think so. Why? Did she say something, and I didn't hear?"

I shook my head. "No, she just…"

He picked up his coke and cocked a brow at me, then smirked.

I wrinkled my nose and took a sip of my wine. "Shut up."

He raised his brows and spread his hands before him, palms up. "I didn't say anything."

"You don't need to."

"It's cute."

I scowled at him. "I said—"

"I didn't notice because I'm not looking," he interrupted. "I've got everything I want right in front of me."

I looked down at the menu to avoid his gaze but didn't bother to read it.

"Are you ready to order?" a female voice said behind me, saving me from the embarrassment of responding to that statement.

"Yes," Jase answered. "I'll have the penne with a garlic bread side." Then he looked at me. "Do you know what you'd like?"

I looked at him in confusion. "Umm, I didn't … I'll have the same, thanks."

"Any sides?"

I shook my head.

"That's everything, thanks," he said, flashing her an enigmatic smile. I set my jaw as she flicked her hair and flounced away, and he laughed.

"That's really not funny."

He sat back and studied me, eyes fixed on my mouth, his thumb running over his bottom lip

"What?"

He turned his mouth down in the corners and cocked his head. "I glanced, I wasn't impressed."

I took another mouthful of wine. "So why are you looking at me like that?"

"I'll show you later."

I put my glass down and tucked my hair behind my ears, trying to contain the thrill that shot through me. All that did was draw my attention to how turned on I was, and I shifted uncomfortably.

I could tell by his expression that he knew. I didn't know how I was supposed to get through a meal feeling like this and necked my drink.

"Another?"

I wasn't sure if he was trying to get me drunk, but I answered, "Umm... yeah."

He flagged down the waitress again, and I watched his hand as he raised it and used two fingers to beckon her over.

I glared at him. "You really need to stop."

"I have no idea what you mean," he said, looking amused.

I stopped talking and wondered why I hadn't just suggested we go straight back to his hotel.

## CHAPTER FOURTEEN

*I* didn't ask him to turn off the light. I wanted to, but that would defeat the whole object of his little exercise. If I were being honest, I was curious as to what exactly he was planning to achieve that he hadn't already. That morning in the shower had been brilliant.

It was strange walking in from dinner with sex planned out. I'd never done that before.

"What are you going to do?"

"Do you want a blow-by-blow account, or can we just see how it goes?"

I pressed my lips together and tried not to laugh as he unzipped my dress, kissing my neck.

"Sorry."

"Don't be nervous."

His low voice behind my ear made me shudder, and he followed the sensation with his fingers down my shoulders, catching my dress and pulling it over my hips, letting it slide to the floor.

"I can't help it."

"How many times have we been here?" he asked, turning me to face him. My head was down, and he lifted my chin gently with his left index finger. "This isn't new. It's you and me together, like we have been dozens of times before. There was just an extended intermission, that's all."

He didn't give me any more time to think, running that finger down my front until he reached my navel, and then he took me by the waist. He stepped closer, his shirt cold and crisp against my bare skin, and reached for the back of my neck with his free hand.

Pulling me close, he lowered his head and kissed me.

He'd never kissed me like this before, no one had, and I was instantly lost in him. In the way his mouth moved, teasing my lips apart to allow his tongue to caress mine. All my trepidation dissipated, and my body began to respond. It responded in ways I'd never known it to, starting with a spasm deep in my core.

"I want to make you feel good," he murmured, breaking his kiss and cupping the side of my face. His eyes searched mine, a request. I knew he could. I believed it was his only goal. And while I didn't fully understand it, I wanted to. I wanted to feel what I'd felt that morning, what he managed to draw from me after so many years of being without it. "Can you trust me enough? One word and I'll stop. Nothing happens you don't feel comfortable with."

I would usually have felt exposed, self-conscious. But something had changed in me. I wasn't afraid. The way he was looking at me as I stood before him in just a bra and panties, made me feel almost worthy of what he wanted to give me. For whatever reason, he wanted me. However damaged. However scarred. He was asking for the one thing I had to give. I reached for him, pulling him to me with his shirt, and he kissed me again briefly before stepping away.

"Lie down."

"Where?"

"Wherever you're comfortable."

He watched me crawl onto the bed, and I glanced over my shoulder to see him unbutton his shirt. He caught me looking, and his expression changed. There was something primal in the way his eyes narrowed and my skin prickled.

I wasn't sure where to position myself, but he moved around the bed, and I had to turn over to see him. I ended up on my side, watching as he unfastened the top two buttons of his jeans and reached into his back pocket.

"Do you want the lights off?" he asked, producing an eye mask.

I wasn't sure. Would not being able to see him make me less conscious of the fact that he would be looking at all of me, or would it make me more aware?

"If you don't like it, I'll take it off."

I wet my lips with my tongue, and his eyes flicked to my mouth. When he tilted his head in question I nodded, and then grinned as he knelt on the edge of the bed and flicked up his chin.

I sat up, allowing him to place the mask over my head, adjusting it gently to cover my eyes. His lips brushed mine, and then he was gone. Gone from the bed. Silent. I strained to hear movement, any indication of where he was and what he was doing, but there was nothing.

Then something brushed my cheek. Soft and light, it tickled as it passed over my skin and down my neck. My head tilted back of its own accord, my intake of breath loud in my ears as the sensation traveled down between my breasts before trailing away.

More silence. I didn't hear him move, breathe, or anything, then the tingles began on the soles of my feet. It didn't tickle in an unpleasant way, more like a gentle breeze passing over my skin, and my toes curled as he passed up and down a couple of times. There was a brief pause, then a different feeling, harder, but still light, running up the centre of my sole. I jumped, then relaxed as the point ran along my ankle and up the inside of my leg to the knee.

"Feather."

He laid it across my stomach, and he settled on the bed at my side.

"I'm going to need you to keep these," his hands pushed and pulled at my knees, parting them, "like this. And I need," his hands left my legs and I was left to anticipate his next move, and then he traced the lace edge of my with his fingertips, "these."

He pulled the cups down, freeing both breasts and leaving them exposed. My nipples hardened in anticipation of his touch, and the seconds ticked by with agonizing slowness as I waited for him. I wasn't disappointed when his tongue circled one, then the other, his hand running over my panties to massage my clit.

"Shit."

I panicked. "What's wrong?"

My knees pulled together, and he nudged them apart. "Keep them there. I didn't expect you to be that wet yet, that's all."

"Sorry."

His hand pulled my underwear to one side, and the cool air of the room chilled my slick folds as he ran his finger along me, gliding up and down, but never reaching my clit. I gasped, rolling my hips, then groaned as he removed his finger entirely. Unable to see him, I wasn't expecting that finger to run along my bottom lip. Instinctively I parted my lips, allowing him to slide his finger into my mouth. "Don't… This is how I want you. Don't ever be sorry," he said as I ran my tongue over his finger, tasting myself.

He withdrew his finger, replacing it with his mouth and kissed me hard. I arched my back and sighed when his chest pressed against my skin, but it was short-lived. He moved away quickly, positioning himself between my legs, and I tried to hook a foot behind his back to pull him toward me.

There was a humming sound that filled the room, and my whole body tensed. He splayed one of his hands on my stomach, then pressed the massager to my clit. It was a few seconds before the effect registered, but when it did, I sucked in a breath and stifled the sound that threatened to burst from my mouth. I tried to fight it, to stop my body from writhing, to keep my legs where he'd put them, but it was too much. I shifted my hips, trying to move it away, to relieve the building tension in my core, but he followed, refusing to let up. Then, just before I drowned in the mix of sensations, he pulled it away.

"Oh, my god…"

He tugged off my panties, and I bent my legs to help him remove them before he placed my legs on either side of his waist and pulled me down the bed. I could tell he was looking at me, studying the parts of me I never exposed. All it did was enhance my arousal.

"Let it out."

I didn't know what he meant, but the rounded edge of the massager ran over the hardened tips of my nipples and my internal muscles clenched. My body knew, even if my brain was uncertain, and my hips raised, legs tightening around his waist, begging him to bring it lower.

The buzzing sound raised in pitch, then he pressed it to my clit and held it firmly in place. It was too much. I couldn't process the sensations and was desperate for some kind of release, for more, or less, or for it to just stop. Desperate for something to do with my hands, I reached for my breasts and squeezed, setting off a reaction I'd never experienced before. My pulse was loud in my ears, and it drowned out the sound of my voice as I came. He took the massager away immediately and lifted my hips. What came next was his name. I gasped it over and over when he closed his mouth over my clit and sucked hard, then released and licked, and massaged that most intimate part of me with his tongue. He kept me on the edge for what seemed like minutes as my body shook with the waves of pleasure he'd drawn from me.

With little warning, he moved over me and kissed my mouth, his cock sliding into me with no effort at all. He kissed, and he thrust, and I reached for his face as he ground into me. I was falling again, only this time I could touch him, and I curled my fingers into his shoulders as another wave of heat surged in my veins. I reveled in every contraction of my muscles around the hard length of him, and every answering movement of his hips as he climbed to his own climax. With one final thrust he came, the power of it almost painful as he buried his hand in my hair and held me against his heaving chest.

Behind the mask, I closed my eyes and breathed in his scent. Our scent. I contracted around him again and he withdrew, kissing me softly and pushing up the mask.

"Okay?"

I took a breath and grinned.

His eyes scanned my face for any sign of distress. "You're sure?"

"I," I pushed up from the bed and kissed him, "have never been better."

There was relief in his smile. I hadn't realized he had reservations. That he was concerned about me, and how I would handle what he wanted to do. "Okay."

He kissed me again then lay at my side, offering his arm for me to rest my head on.

He held me all night, just like that. I listened to his soft breathing for a while after he fell asleep, enjoying the warmth of his body and smiling at the occasional twitch of his fingers where they rested along my waist. But I couldn't keep the darker thoughts away. They crept in, and I eventually fell asleep wondering what was coming. Something had to be. I couldn't be this happy without repercussions. There was always a trade-off. That was how my life worked. The good-bad balance never tipped to the good side for long. I worried I was on borrowed time with him.

## CHAPTER FIFTEEN

It was Sunday night and Haylie lay on my sofa with her head in my lap. Our default set up when she and Tommo had a falling out. I was absentmindedly stroking her hair, watching the film, when out of nowhere she said, "This is a load of shit."

I couldn't have agreed more. "You chose it."

"Yeah. Can't seem to get anything right."

I pressed my lips into a grim line and looked down at her. "I'm sorry."

She pushed herself up and faced me, crossing her legs. As much as she tried to look angry, she was failing in her penguin onesie. "Fuck him. What did you do this weekend?"

I leaned over and picked up my mug, the unicorn hood of my very bright onesie falling over my head. "Not much. Dinner. Shopping… you know."

"Oooh… did he splash the cash?"

I knew I shouldn't have said anything. I was a bad liar at the best of times, and she'd only ask to see any items I said he'd bought, regardless of their intimate nature.

I stalled for time, taking a big sip of my hot chocolate, but she was glaring at me, waiting for my reply. I lowered the mug and hugged it. "Sort of…"

"Where did he take you?"

I closed my eyes and exhaled. "To a sex shop for a fuck load of toys. I didn't know half of that shit existed, but the ones we've tried so far are…" I gave her a very cheesy grin. It said what I couldn't. "He's breaking me in gently, he said."

Her expression was worth my discomfort. "You? What? How?"

I shrugged. "I was nervous. I faked it, and he called me out. I didn't have a choice but to tell him the truth."

She was looking at me like I was mad. "Truth being?"

"That I hadn't had a good orgasm for years. And years. He's made it his personal mission to make sure I get off."

"But you don't… You've never been one for… Fucking hell, Nat."

"I can learn… apparently."

"What, so he's gone all Obi Wan on you?"

I burst out laughing. "That's sick. He just likes… Well, that's his business. Safe to say I have extra packing to do every other weekend."

She was shaking her head. "You mean to tell me he hasn't stayed here yet in… Shit, it's been a month."

I shrugged and looked around the room. "It'd be weird."

She knew what I was getting at, and I knew she wouldn't have it. "There isn't a damn thing left in here from when you were married. I even helped you rip the kitchen out. That bed has never been shagged in. Not once. It's been a complete waste of the three hours it took to build the damn thing."

"Once…" I said weakly.

"That was shit. Shit sex doesn't count," she said, getting off the sofa and digging in her pocket for her cigarettes. "If you're jumping into this whole new lifestyle you should get a few nights of it in your own bed."

I stayed where I was while she went to the back door to smoke.

"When are you going to his actual house anyway?" she shouted.

I could smell the smoke drifting through the house, so I took my mug and closed the living room door behind me, joining her outside.

"We haven't gotten there yet. Right now, it's hotel rooms and not rushing anything. I'm not traveling down to his place when he hasn't even stayed in my house. We haven't discussed any of this yet, anyway."

She choked on cigarette smoke as she laughed. "But you can go out shopping for dildos and butt plugs?"

I resisted the urge to slam the door on her and lock her in the garden. "I'm going to bed."

"I'll be up in ten. Set your alarm, I sleep through mine."

I went upstairs, wondering how that could possibly be a problem since her phone had the same alert tones mine did, and she could just change it. I wouldn't ask. Those were never good questions to ask Haylie. By the time I'd cleaned my teeth and set my alarm, my thoughts turned back to Jase. I realized he hadn't contacted me at all that evening, and he left just after lunch, so I turned off the bedroom light and sent a quick goodnight message as I climbed into bed.

His reply arrived at the same time as Haylie. She wandered round the bed and pushed the window open.

"Aww," she cooed.

"What?"

She put on a soppy voice. "Love you. Love you too. Thanks for the rabbit, I love it."

I put my phone down and turned my back to her as she got into my bed. "You're a dickhead."

She snuggled into my back, put her arm around my waist, and squeezed. "Yeah, but I'm your dickhead. Thanks for letting me stay. Even though I hate being the big spoon."

"That's too much. Seriously, how are you so warm?"

She clicked her tongue. "You're still in that stupid onesie, genius."

I groaned. "You're naked, aren't you?"

She planted a sloppy kiss on my cheek and turned over. "Night."

I got into work on time. Strangely, there was no sign of Sandra. I went to her desk to see if she'd left any notes for me but there was nothing, so I checked my email. I was replying to the first when Tony stuck his head out of his office door and said, "Nathalie, can I have a word?"

Chantal was looking at me over her monitor. Rachel, the other co-worker I hadn't bothered to get to know, gave me a side glance as I got up from my chair and nodded my head. They watched me step inside, and Tony groaned as he closed the door behind me.

"Sit down, Nathalie."

My stomach churned, making me feel sick. "What's wrong?"

He sat in his chair opposite me and leaned his elbows on the desk. "There have been a few developments. Sandra was in an accident over the weekend and is expected to be off for the foreseeable future. Damage to her back, severe sciatic pain. She won't be fit to sit at a desk. As the most qualified person in the office, I'd be incredibly grateful if you could take over her duties."

I blinked. I was relieved it wasn't about the inappropriate relationship I had with a company director, but I was shocked at the instant promotion thrown in with the news, and I needed a second to get my head together.

"You want me to do her job? I…"

"That isn't all. I'm afraid I'm going to need you to train Chantal to do your job while you're at it."

My brows must have risen because he chuckled. I tried to school my features and said, "Sorry Tony, it's just… Well, with me and… What about Rachel?"

He looked at his computer screen and clicked his mouse a couple of times. "She's already doing much of what you do. That's her job. You're more qualified than even Sandra is, so I know you can meet the challenge. Truth be told, you're the better candidate, she just applied and was set on before you sent in your resume."

"I don't know… I mean… You know about Jason and me, don't you?"

He sat back, sighed, and looked at me. "He's my oldest friend and business partner. Yes, I'm aware of your relationship with Jason. Does your personal life affect your performance at work?"

"No..."

"Are you likely to bring your personal life into work at any point? Considering the distance between the two offices, and that Jason works in various locations around the country most weeks?"

"No, but..."

"Have you disclosed information about your relationship with Jason to any of the staff here?"

The thought of telling that pair of harpies anything about my life, let alone about Jase, was absurd. "Absolutely not."

"Then why are you thinking about this? I need a temporary business manager. You're qualified to fill the position. You'll receive the pay increase and benefits due while you fill the position. And should the position become available indefinitely, it will not be advertised. I can transfer all the necessary files from Sandra's computer to yours from here. I'm afraid that makes you responsible for handling the payroll information for this office, emailing it to the Cambridge office on Thursday mornings by ten, but it shouldn't be anything like your last position. Delegate to Rachel where necessary, Chantal will require some supervision."

"Okay, can I just—"

"No is not an option."

I frowned. "I was going to say thank you..."

He grinned at me, his eyes crinkling in the corners. "Thank you. You're saving me a lot of work in finding a replacement for Sandra. I'll let Jason know."

I nodded and sat there for a moment. I needed to explain myself. I wasn't sure how much Jason had told him, but I wanted to be clear. Just before I lost my nerve, I blurted, "I honestly didn't know, you know."

He gave me a reassuring smile. I liked that about him, that he always seemed to consider how his actions would be received. "I know. It was unfortunate that you discovered his involvement here the way you did, but I think in the long run, it'll turn out to have been a blessing."

I had no way of knowing just how much Jason had told him. "It isn't serious."

He smiled. "Perhaps not yet, but I know Jason. Can you tell Chantal I'd like a word, please?"

I nodded and stood up, that statement resonating in my ears. "Umm... tea?"

He looked relieved I'd offered because he never usually asked. "Oh, please. Two sugars."

I walked out of there wondering what had just happened, stopping by Chantal's desk and murmuring Tony's request before heading into the staff room. I made tea for Tony, coffee for me, and knocked on the window facing into the office miming "brew?" to Rachel. She gave me a blank look and went back to whatever she was doing. I decided that was the last time I'd offer, and delivered Tony's drink. He thanked me but didn't look up from his computer, and I left him to it.

I could feel Chantal's eyes on me as I passed her, whatever he'd said to her was clearly pissing her off. I sat down, glanced up at her, then over to Rachel before opening my emails. I didn't give a shit what either of them thought. Poor Sandra was ill, and someone had to do her job. I was just helping Tony out.

There, at the top of my inbox, was one from J Locksley. I opened it.

*Morning Beautiful,*
*Congratulations, T just told me. I'm out of the office but will call tonight.*
*Jase*

I pressed my lips together, trying to hide the smile, and hit reply.

*Mr. Locksley,*
*Thank you. It was a pleasant surprise.*
*Apologies, but it seems you have confused my personal and work email addresses. Please only contact me via previously agreed channels.*
*Many thanks,*
*N Johnson*
*Admin Manager*

My phone vibrated on my desk, and I turned it over to see a message from Jason. Just an eye roll emoji, nothing more.

I managed not to laugh and turned the phone over, screen down, so I couldn't be distracted by any more messages.

When lunch time arrived, I snatched it up and went straight into the staff room to eat my lunch and call Haylie to share my good news.

"No, Jase had nothing to do with it," I said when she started asking stupid questions.

"Sure?"

"Yes, I'm sure. You staying at mine again tonight? I'll buy dinner to celebrate."

"Could I?" she asked. "If he's on one again I might kill him."

I shook my head and smiled. Her turbulent relationship with her boyfriend didn't last long in either direction. Their squabbles were soon forgotten, just as their times of apparent contentment with one another were short-lived. But that was them. They'd been the same way for a decade, and I was sure they wouldn't be changing. It worked for them in its own weird way.

"Course you can. He won't have gone anywhere else, he bloody lives there. Give it a couple of days, and it'll all blow over. It's not like I don't need the company, is it?"

"Cheers. I'll pick up the wine on the way back."

"Just one bottle," I warned. "I can't come in hungover the day after I get a promotion."

The door opened behind me, and I cut the call short. "Okay, I have to go, see you tonight. Bye." Rachel closed the door quietly behind her, and I smiled. "Hiya."

She looked me up and down and went to the fridge. "I hear you've taken Sandy's job already."

"No," I responded, surprised. "I'm taking over from her while she's off, just as Chantal is taking over from me."

She shrugged, taking her lunch out and closing the door. "That's not how Chantal told it."

I wanted to say something to her about whispers spreading lies, but I thought better of it. "She's mistaken. As soon as Sandra comes back, I'll be back to basic admin."

"Would have been nice to be considered," she muttered, looking uncomfortable.

Then I understood. I was annoyed with Chantal for her insensitivity but masked it as I tried to explain. "I was only asked to do it because I have a managerial degree. I don't really like working in management, found out a bit late, that's why I took the position I did. It's temporary. I only accepted so Tony wouldn't have to bring in a temp. We don't need that, we've only just got settled ourselves, haven't we?" I gave what I hoped was a reassuring smile.

She looked a bit embarrassed. "Oh. It's just how Chantal said… Never mind. I hope Sandy's okay."

It seemed odd hearing Rachel refer to her so informally, it reminded me that I wasn't part of their team. Not really. "Yeah. Tony didn't give me any details, but he sounded as though he expected her to be back."

She nodded her head and sat down opposite me. "We should send her some flowers or something."

"Yeah. I'll sort that with Tony later. What are you thinking, ten each?"

She nodded and opened her lunch. "Salad for a change."

I laughed and waved my tub at her. "Yep. I tell myself I like it and treat myself with a biscuit at three."

The door opened again and two of the engineers walked in. I didn't remember all of their names, they weren't in the office that often, choosing to keep to the workshop, so I didn't get to talk to them, but I recognized them.

"All right, love?" the older of the two asked as the younger nodded.

I smiled. Rachel frowned at me and dug into her lunch as I tried not to overhear their conversation.

"Don't worry about it," the older one said, I was sure he was called Paul. "It's his tech, he'll come and sort it."

"Won't he be pissed we can't get it moving?" the other asked. I recognised him from the interviews. Matt.

"Nah," Paul said, filling the kettle. "He'd rather come up and deal with it than there be an accident. I've been with the company since they first started and believe me, Jay doesn't mind getting his hands dirty."

"Everything okay?" I asked conversationally.

"Yeah. Burst pipe right in the middle of town. Traffic's backed up in both directions. I had to call Jay in."

Rachel looked at him, confused. "Jay?"

"Mister Locksley," Paul clarified. "Engineering Director."

My phone rang. I looked around them and flushed. "Excuse me."

I tried not to run out of the staff room and into the bathroom as I answered. "Hello?"

"It's me. I'm coming back up there. Now. If I get finished early enough can I see you? I haven't booked a room yet, but when I have somewhere, I'll book under your name so you can get the keys."

My earlier conversation with Haylie popped into my head. Whether it was a good idea or not I wasn't sure, but I said, "You could just stay with me."

I could tell he was grinning. "That works. I have to go, my phone's going mental. I'll keep you posted."

"Okay… Umm, see you later then?"

"I'll make sure you do."

I was smiling like an idiot when he hung up. For all of ten seconds, when I remembered Haylie. "Shit…"

Three clicks and the dial tone started. "Yeah?"

"I'm so sorry… You can't stay. He's coming back, and I told him to stay with me. I didn't think, I'm sorry. Will you be okay?"

"Oh, my god. At your house?"

I knew she couldn't see me, but I pulled a face. "Yes, at my house. Where else?"

"Wow… Okay."

"Will you be okay?"

"Yeah… I'll break out the big guns."

I wasn't sure I wanted to know, but I said, "Yeah?"

"Hmm. I can't tell you how much I hate *Top Gun*, but I'll cook his favorite and sit through it." I tried so hard not to laugh that it came out as a snort. "I want all the gory details."

"Bye, Hayles."

"All of them!" she shouted as I took the phone away from my ear.

"Love you."

I hung up and went back to my salad. Rachel was waiting for me when I got back, a fresh cup of coffee sitting on the table.

"Okay?" she asked as I sat down.

"Yeah, perfect. Thanks." I took a sip of the coffee, and she smiled.

## CHAPTER SIXTEEN

There was a gentle knock on the door at nine thirty.

"I was expecting you to be much later. Go through," I said, closing the door behind him.

He looked up at the staircase, then to the right, into the living room. "Yeah. The rig was faulty. I brought a spare with me and got it sealed. I've been up to the office for a shower and got changed before I came here."

I followed him in, giving him time to look around. I assumed he was looking for evidence of my previous life. Of him. He wouldn't find any. "Are you hungry?"

He shook his head. "No. Thanks. And thanks for letting me..." He trailed off.

"It was about time," I replied, moving around him and to the door at the other end of the room. "Drink?"

He followed me into the kitchen. "Yeah. The house is nice."

I laughed quietly, taking two glasses from the cupboard and opening the fridge for a bottle of wine. "Took a while, but I made it just mine. More or less."

He watched me pour the wine and took the glass when I offered it. "Tony said you didn't want the job at first."

I shrugged. "I didn't think it was right… I mean…"

"He said."

I didn't know how much they shared and didn't bother to ask. "He set me straight. It won't be for long, he expects her back from the way he was talking."

He nodded and sipped the wine, looking around the room. "I hope I haven't messed with your plans tonight. I know it was short notice."

I shook my head. "No, honestly it's fine. Haylie was staying, but she's probably better off sorting her messy relationship out. Death by *Top Gun* isn't the best way to go, but that isn't my problem."

He gave me a quizzical look, and I laughed, shaking my head. "Doesn't matter. Come through."

He joined me on the sofa. "Is there a reason you have no photographs?" he asked, looking around. "Or ornaments. Not even a potted plant…"

"No. I don't like reminders, and I don't do plants or flowers. I forget to water them and don't really like watching stuff die."

He gave me an odd look and asked, "So buying flowers is a no?"

"I don't think there's anything nice about it. *I killed this for you, have fun watching it rot.*"

"Fair enough," he said, I assumed making a mental note.

"I have some things. I call it my Morbid Box," I mutter, feeling like I had to give some sort of explanation. "It only comes out on very special occasions. Want to see it?"

He took a drink and answered, "If this is a special occasion, then I'd love to."

He was watching me. I could see he was tired, but he was genuinely interested.

I shrugged. "Suppose it is. I'll be back in a minute."

I left him sitting on the couch and went into the kitchen, dragging a chair from the small table and using it to stand on so I could reach the top of the cupboard.

The box was covered in dust, and I made a mental note to clean the cupboards as I took a damp cloth from the sink and wiped it off. I drank my wine in three gulps and refilled the glass before going back into the living room. I held it out to him and said, "Here you go, knock yourself out."

He looked at it for a second then opened it. I curled up on the sofa and watched him, sipping my wine as he pulled out the first stack of photographs. Each had a small note attached, and I waited for his reaction as he lifted the slip of paper to view the image beneath.

"Mum took these, but they're the same as the ones used as evidence," I explained as he looked, read, and carefully placed it on the sofa arm.

He didn't say anything, moving through the photos showing the injuries I'd sustained in all their horrific glory. He stared at the picture of me in the wheelchair with my leg in a huge cast much longer than the others.

"How long were you in the…" He swallowed, not finishing the sentence.

"A few months. Obviously, the screws did their job, but it took a long time. I was out of the cast as soon as possible so I could get moving. I gained a lot of weight sitting on my arse for all that time. The physical therapy I had with the cast on wasn't enough."

"You were nearly killed, and you're hung up on the weight you gained?" he asked in disbelief.

I shrugged again. "It was the one thing I thought I could change after. The scars were always going to be there, but the weight I could get rid of."

I could see the sadness in his eyes and craned my neck to see the next photo. "That was the day they woke me up. They put me in an induced coma because of the knock to the head when I landed… Mum and Haylie filled the room with balloons. It was like coming 'round in a ball pit."

He smiled at the photo now in his hand. "How is your mum?"

I took a steadying breath and picked up the pictures he'd already looked at. "She passed two years ago. Cancer."

His brows pulled together, and he passed me the photograph. He paused at the next one.

"Cost a damn fortune to get me looking like that," I said with a humorless laugh. "It was a good day, considering."

"This is how I remembered you."

I shook my head. "I'd changed a lot by then. That's the only one left of the wedding. I was going to cut him out of it but never got around to it. Mum said it was good to remember something positive about him. I try not to remember anything at all most days, but…"

He put the photos back in the box and handed it to me. "Thank you, for sharing those with me. I'm sorry about your mum, she was always…"

"Yeah. She was pretty amazing. I know it sounds weird, but I try not to think about her too much. I miss her less that way." I put the pictures back in the box and dropped it on the floor at my feet, then reached for my bag. Pulling my purse out, I opened it and handed it to him. "But I do keep her picture with me all the time."

But he wasn't looking at that. His attention was fixed on the small charm hanging from the zip of the coin compartment. Two tiny brass keys hanging from a clasp. "You kept them?"

I chewed the inside of my cheek as he looked at me.

"Do you remember when we found them?"

I smiled at the memory. It was the coldest Saturday in June on record and we decided to take the train to the coast. We sheltered from the rain beneath the pier and he plucked them from the sand.

"I can't believe you still have them. That you kept them."

I drained my glass and put it down on top of the Morbid Box. "Of course, I did. They helped me get through some really shitty days to be honest."

He closed the purse and handed it back to me. "In what way?"

I smiled. "I had a lot of good memories to look back at. On hopeless days, I thought about them and told myself I could get there again, eventually. If I just took the step. If I managed without the crutches. If I got back to normal, I could meet someone, I could have a life." *With someone who loved me*, I finished in my head. Because deep down I really believed I was worthy of it, regardless of the shit hands I'd been dealt so far.

"You know I wouldn't do anything to hurt you, don't you? You know you can trust me?" he asked.

I wasn't ready for that question. I knew the answer. I was almost certain I knew he wouldn't, not physically at least, but there was a part of me that couldn't answer because he couldn't know. "I trust that you wouldn't run me over," I said. "But shit happens. All I'm ever going to ask of you is that you're honest. I'm sorry, but I can't give you another answer."

He reached for my hand and gave it a gentle squeeze. I relaxed and stifled a yawn.

"Shall we go to bed?"

I looked up at the clock. "Probably should. I've got a lot to sort tomorrow. Sandra's files are a complete mess and I have no idea how she finds anything."

Grinning at me, he stood up and pulled me to my feet. "How does it feel being on the management team?"

"I'll let you know on payday," I teased, pulling my hand away and picking up our glasses. "Bathroom's at the top of the stairs, my room second right. I'll be up in a minute."

He kissed me and went upstairs while I cleaned up. I was glad to shove my Morbid Box back on top of the cupboard, out of sight and out of mind.

I could hear him moving around upstairs. It felt off having someone in the house who wasn't Haylie. I wasn't sure what to do about it. After a couple of minutes, I settled on doing nothing and checked the back door, removed the key, and put it in the cutlery drawer. I turned off the lights and made sure the front door was secure before heading upstairs myself.

He was sitting on the edge of my bed when I got in there, and when he saw me he held out his hands. I took them, letting him pull me into his arms. With his head on my stomach, he took a deep breath. I combed my fingers through his hair and kissed the top of his head.

"Come on, let's get some sleep," I murmured eventually, stepping out of his embrace. "You've got to drive south again tomorrow, and I have to train Chantal to do my job while I'm doing someone else's."

* * *

I woke up alone. The bed was still warm on the opposite side, so he hadn't been gone long. I lay quietly, listening. The radio was on downstairs. I smiled, relieved he hadn't done a runner, and climbed out of bed, reaching for my bathrobe.

I found him in the kitchen. Singing. He'd made toast and coffee and was getting the butter out of the fridge when he saw me leaning against the doorframe watching him.

"So, you sing?"

He smiled, reaching for me with his free hand and dragging me toward him by the belt of my robe. "Only on very special occasions," he said, kissing me. "Breakfast is ready."

He moved to the table, pulling out a chair for me, while I reached for my coffee and asked, "What's special about today?"

"We had our first sleepover."

I chuckled into my mug. "We've had lots of sleepovers."

He shook his head and buttered me a slice of toast. "Hotels don't count." Dropping the slice onto my plate, he reached for another and buttered that. "This is different."

"So, we're celebrating this momentous occasion with toast and singing?"

"Is there a better way?"

I took a bite of my toast and shook my head. "Nope. This is perfect. Thank you."

We ate, I got dressed, and I followed him to work. Tony wasn't in yet, but the cleaner was just leaving, and she held the door for us. I thanked her and went straight into the office, and turned on the computer while he made us both a drink.

"I need to check something in the workshop. I'll let you know when I leave, and I'll call tonight," he said, leaning over and kissing my cheek as I sat at my desk.

I smiled, resting my head back against his abdomen. "Thanks for staying. And for breakfast."

"Thank you for letting me stay. We'll have to do it again some time."

I smiled. "Yeah. Hotels are nice for a change but there's something about being at home."

He kissed my forehead and stepped back. "Yeah… Oh. Good morning, Chantal, is it?"

My stomach clenched. "Shit…"

It was barely a whisper. But he heard me and placed his hand on my shoulder. It was supposed to reassure me, but I panicked and shrugged it off, flashing her an awkward smile. "Morning."

She looked at us both, then went straight into the staff room with her phone in her hand. I sagged into my seat. "Crap."

He didn't seem concerned. "Don't worry about it."

"That's easy for you to say," I hissed, looking back at the staff room door. "You're her bloody boss."

He chuckled. "So are you now," he said with a wink. "Have fun. I'll see you later."

I scowled at the back of his head as he sauntered off toward the door that led to the workshop, feeling a little bit sick at the prospect of spending the day working closely with Chantal after she'd caught us.

## CHAPTER SEVENTEEN

Three days had passed, and I couldn't have been more relieved to see a Friday. Chantal had wasted no time in sharing her discovery with Rachel, and naturally she'd gone quiet on me again. I wasn't devastated, it wasn't as though we'd been friends of any sort, but it had been nice to have someone to speaking with at work for a few short hours. The news had reached the engineers too, and I received more than one knowing look and tip of the head before the week was through.

By the time I sorted all my stuff, Tony and I were the only ones left in the building. I grabbed my bag and stopped by his open door on my way out. "Have a good weekend."

"You too. And thank you for this week. You have no idea how much of a help you've been."

He was at his desk, shirt undone at the neck, one hand rubbing the back of his neck. He looked exhausted. "Is there anything else you need before I go home?"

He shook his head and smiled up at me. "No, really." He looked at me for a moment then said, "Forgive me if I'm speaking out of turn, Nathalie, but can I just take a moment to thank you for your influence elsewhere?"

I look at him in confusion.

"Jason," he clarified. "The change in him recently is, well, he's a different bloke, and I have you to thank for that. He's my oldest friend, and while there hasn't been the opportunity for us to get to know one another outside of work, I hope we get the chance soon."

I wasn't sure what to say. I didn't know how to measure any change in Jason since I didn't know him that well anymore, but I was pleased he seemed happy with me. "Yeah. We should probably arrange something with Jase next time he's up... Whenever that will be."

His eyes twinkled as his smile broadened. "I will. See you on Monday."

I smiled, hitched my bag onto my shoulder, and left the building feeling a little flat. Mentioning Jason made me miss him. I had the weekend to get through without him and the prospect wasn't a happy one. I sat in my car and pulled out my phone.

"What's the plan this weekend?"

"We're going to get smashed."

"Oh, dear... What happened?" I put my phone on speaker and started my car.

"Tuesday night was fine, then Wednesday morning he was in a mood again. I don't know what's wrong with him. I'd kick him out if he had somewhere to go, I swear."

I left the industrial park and turned onto the main road. "Okay. Come to me, I'll cook. I'll go in for stuff now and be home around six."

She agreed and hung up. I made my way to the supermarket for supplies.

I was cooking dinner while we discussed our week. I'd gotten to the part where Chantal had seen me and Jason on Monday morning, and after giving me hell for not calling her after a rough day, regardless of how busy she was with work, Haylie responded as I expected.

"So, she went around and told everyone? Little bitch," she raged as she opened a bottle of vodka. "You should have her for it."

I shook my head and stirred the sauce I was making. "There's no point. To be fair, it does look set up. I said it myself. Tony didn't seem bothered, and Jase says he had nothing to do with it, but I knew how it looked before I accepted."

"Doesn't sound like Tony gave you a choice." She handed me a vodka and orange. "What's he like, anyway?"

"He's nice," I said, turning off the hob and moving my attention to layering pasta and sauces in a deep dish. "I haven't really spoken to him except to hand over paperwork and stuff like that. He did stop me today though, told me Jason had changed recently and thanked me for it. I don't know what it has to do with me, but Tony seems to think I'm a positive part of his life."

"So, he doesn't care his mate is bedding his Admin Manager?"

I snorted and threw the two empty saucepans in the dishwasher, then took a gulp of my drink. "Nope. Apparently not. Said he'd like to get to know me better, or words to that effect."

She slid up onto the worktop and her mouth pulled down in the corners. I was expecting something altogether more inappropriate, but she said, "Well if you get the friend's blessing, you're golden."

I glanced at her and raised my eyebrows. "Yeah?"

"Definitely," she affirmed with a stern nod. "Jason's got mine, you have Tony's. You're set."

"Oh, well if you give us the green light, I'm sure it'll all work out perfectly," I teased. "Pass me the cheese."

"Do you think that's why me and Tommo have such a hard time?"

"What?"

She passed me the cheese and returned to the worktop. "Well, his mates don't bother with me. You don't bother with him."

"Now hang on," I protested, nearly grating my thumb when I looked around at her. "I invite him over all the time. He's the one not bothering. And when I come over to yours, I just get grunts and sighs because I'm interrupting his very important model building. It's not like I haven't tried with him, Hayles. He just doesn't like me."

"He doesn't not like you, he just doesn't know what to say to you," she replied gloomily. "He was shocked when… that happened. First, he was angry, then he was upset it happened to you, and then he just didn't know how to approach you after you got better. He sent me over all the time. I was worried I was suffocating you, but he kept on sending me to check."

I frowned, feeling a bit guilty. "Why haven't you told me this before?"

She shrugged and drained her glass. "I dunno. It didn't seem important."

I set the timer on the oven, slid the lasagna in, and poured myself another drink. "I thought he was a wanker for years. It was important."

"I thought Jason was a wanker for years, but look—"

"You pushed me to see him!" I said with exasperation.

"To get him out of your system. I didn't know you were going to fall for him all over again."

"I haven't… I didn't."

She looked at me with her brows raised and her lips pulled to one side.

"Shit." I wasn't ready to process it yet. Saying it out loud made it all so much more real and worse, and Haylie had figured it out.

She started cackling. I went into the living room. "You didn't work that out?" she asked, hopping onto the sofa next to me. "What did you think it was, a booty call on redial?"

"Well, no, but I didn't think… Well, this is…"

"What happens when you hop into bed with someone you've loved forever?"

I looked at her. "I'm in trouble, aren't I?"

"No, you're right where you're supposed to be. I'm the one in trouble. Probably."

"You need to talk to him."

She pressed her lips together and nodded her head. "What if he wants to end it?"

I had to be honest. "You won't know until you speak to him. It could be something completely unrelated. Leaving him to it for a bit, letting him work through whatever's going on with him can't hurt. When you do go back and talk, you know he's had some time."

"I don't know what I'm supposed to say."

I shrugged. "It doesn't matter. If you're going to stand a chance, you must communicate."

She looked at me and narrowed her eyes.

"Okay, I stole that. Jase said the same thing to me, and he's right."

"Looks like you're doing a lot of that," she said with a saucy smile.

"We aren't talking about me."

"The shoe fits."

I scowled at her and got up, heading into the kitchen. She didn't follow me, and I was glad. I needed a few minutes. I took the opportunity to fix a salad while the lasagna finished cooking, considering what Haylie had revealed.

I was just plating our meal when she appeared in the kitchen door. "Phone's ringing."

I took it from her and looked at the screen.

"Answer then," she whispered, staring at me.

I shook my head and let it ring off. "I'll call him back later."

She frowned at me, but I smiled. "Dinner's ready."

* * *

I'd had considerably more vodka when he called again.

"Are you okay?" he asked, sounding a little concerned.

"I'm fine. I'm more than fine. What are you doing?"

"Nothing. I had dinner, tried to call you but you didn't answer, now I'm watching TV, bored senseless."

"Sorry, we were having dinner ourselves."

"We?"

"Yes, we. Hayles is staying over. Her boyfriend isn't talking to her, so she came here to keep me company."

"I was thinking. Next weekend, do you want to go somewhere?" he queried.

I went quiet.

"Nat?"

"Sorry, yeah… Like where?"

"Anywhere you want. I'll pick you up, and we can get away for a bit."

"What's brought this on?" I asked as Haylie came into the room, the smell of cigarette smoke and cold air clinging to her onesie. I inhaled as she sat next to me, the old craving making my fingers restless. She rested against me and sighed, the vodka clearly doing its job with her, and I rested my head against hers.

"I was thinking about the other morning, and how good it was just being… Well, just being us."

"We can do that any weekend. It isn't like I need permission to have you over, is it?"

"No, but I wanted to treat you."

"I don't need treating, Jason. I need you."

It was his turn to go quiet.

"I mean… I miss you."

"No, no, I want to be with you more, really, it's just… I've got a lot to handle here, and it isn't something I can just walk away from."

Haylie had fallen asleep, which wasn't surprising, she was drinking doubles to my singles. I shuffled away from her and moved into the kitchen, closing the door. "I'm not asking you to. I just… I don't even know what. I've had a really shit week with one thing and another—"

"You mean the staff has been talking?" he asked, not sounding surprised.

"Well, yeah. The office junior saw you kiss me. She fell over herself to start talking. I don't care, I go in, I do my job, I leave. I'm not there to make friends."

He sighed. "I don't want to cause problems for you at work, babe. But you know it's probably just jealousy. They'll forget about it soon enough."

A familiar sensation fluttered in my stomach and I smiled to myself. He hadn't called me that since we'd started seeing each other again. It was all he called me our first time around. "It's fine. Honestly. What are you doing tomorrow?"

"Oh, this and that. I'll be thinking of you, though."

"Yeah?"

"Yeah. I think of you all the time. I can give you some examples—"

"Don't you dare," I hissed, flushing. "I think about you all the time too… Jase, can I ask you something?"

"Anything."

I glanced at the living room door, then to the back door, and went for it. Haylie had left her smokes on the counter, and I grabbed them and went outside. "What are we doing?"

"I know what I'm doing," he said. "I'm trying to make this long-distance thing work and clearly doing a terrible fucking job of it."

"You're not," I mumbled weakly. "I'm sorry, I just… I need to know where this is going. I don't want… I can't, not again."

He went quiet. I lit a smoke and took a long drag, then closed my eyes as the chemicals gave me a head rush.

"I'm trying so hard, so fucking hard not to fuck this up. You're too important."

I frowned at his words and took another drag.

"I don't want to rush anything, babe."

My eyes welled, and I brushed the tears away with my thumb, smoke from the cigarette making it worse. I sniffed.

"Nat, don't get upset. Please. I…"

"I love you." The three biggest words in the world, and I blurted them out like that.

He was quiet for a few seconds, then cleared his throat. "You know smoking is really bad for you?"

I snorted into the mouthpiece and took another drag. "I only smoke when I'm drunk."

"So, you're drunk, and I'm missing it? Damn."

"Okay, not drunk. But I've had a few vodkas, and it's been a crap week apart from seeing you. I needed a smoke."

"Hmmm," he hummed. "Well, it's late, and you have a bottle to finish from the sounds of it. I'll call you tomorrow."

I smiled. "Okay. Not too early though."

He laughed softly and said, "Sleep well, babe."

His laugh cheered me right up. "Okay."

"I love you, too."

He ended the call before I could respond, but I stood in the garden grinning to myself and flicked the smoke into the corner by the gate. I didn't need the smoke to calm my nerves, I needed to know he felt the same way as me, and he'd said it. I could tell he meant it.

## CHAPTER EIGHTEEN

"Where are we going?" I asked, getting into his car. He'd been waiting outside when I got home from work, and I had to rush to get changed.

"Just for a few drinks. I don't plan to be out too late, I have things I want to do," he said as he fastened his seatbelt and winked at me.

I wasn't about to ask what. "Who with?" I enquired instead.

"Tony. I thought it was time you got to know my friends."

"I already know him," I replied as he pulled slowly out of my street. "I work with him every day."

"Oh, not that Tony, he's a boring arse. The real Tony doesn't wear a suit."

I smirked. "Okay. We need to stop and pick up a bottle of wine or something."

"Nope," he said turning onto the main road out of town. "He only drinks one wine, and I'm not paying for that. I'll pay for dinner."

"What's for dinner?"

"Pizza."

I snorted. "Expensive wine and pizza?"

"Yeah. He was raised with a silver spoon in his mouth, likes the finer things but rebels with junk food. I did my best with him but… well." He shrugged his broad shoulders.

"You're not exactly the lad who left here, Jase," I said seriously. "You did a good job dropping your accent."

"I had to," he disclosed. "I got into one of the most prestigious universities in the country on my own ability, but there was no way I was going to fit in with a working-class accent. I dropped it pretty quickly. It helped sharing a house with Tony, Rich, and Cara."

That was a revelation. "You all lived together?"

He laughed. "Yeah. We came up with the whole business idea the last few months of uni. Well, Cara saw my designs and spoke to her dad. Her dad was impressed. He's big in property, and one of his friends helped me build the prototype models, patent it, and set me up with some connections. Cara pushed Tony to join me, she was always able to talk him into stuff, and even saw how to bring Rich in."

"Rich has been there since day one, too?" I asked. I hadn't met him but had spoken to him a few times on the phone, handling some very urgent samples. He seemed nice.

"He was really important to making the whole thing work, actually. The filter is our bread and butter product, but without him we couldn't test our own samples and the costs were too high to outsource."

"And did Cara talk him around, too?"

He laughed. "No. God, no. Cara was the reason he hesitated. She can be a bit… overbearing, and he doesn't do so well with it."

"I didn't get that from her at all," I mused, looking out the window. We'd left town and were heading out toward a nearby village. "Does he live out here?"

"He missed the country," he said as an explanation. "He grew up in the middle of nowhere. When we needed to expand, he chose this area. I had a connection to the place. Good links to the north of the country, not too urban. He was glad to move up here."

The car slowed, and he turned down a long, pebbled drive.

"Fucking hell," I muttered under my breath.

"What?" he questioned, like there wasn't a damn thing to be impressed at.

"How many bedrooms does that thing have?"

"Seven? I dunno. Watch out for the dogs. They're wild."

I got out of the car and stared at the huge house as the baying of hounds began.

"Jason. Please, don't let them near me."

He heard the panic in my voice and moved around the car, grabbing my hand and pulling me behind him as they came bounding toward us. They were massive, all flapping jowls and wafting ears, and didn't seem to want to slow down, and I could feel a scream building in my throat.

"Sonny, Lurch, no."

The two bloodhounds came to a skidding halt a few feet away, the larger of the two collapsing in a heap and rolling onto his back and wagging his tail. Jase gave my hand a gentle squeeze then let go, approaching the dogs. "All right, calm down. Yeah, I've missed you," he addressed them, going down on his knees and rubbing the belly of the big one as the other jumped on his back. "Shit, Lurch, get down."

I took another step away and reached for the door handle when the big one got up off the ground and started wrestling against Jason's chest, vying for his attention, when a high whistle called them off. They shot back up the drive, and I saw Tony come through a wrought iron gate to the side of the house wearing a pair of shorts, a t-shirt, and no shoes.

Jason got up and turned to me with an apologetic smile. "I should have checked, sorry."

I shook my head. "No, I should have mentioned it. I went off dogs when Gav brought his dad's to ours. His weren't too friendly, hunting dogs, and they bit my hand more than once." I lifted my right hand to point out the few silver lines along my thumb.

I saw a flicker of anger in his eyes and looked away as Tony drew close.

"I'm sorry, Nathalie. I forgot to close the gate."

I shook my head and smiled. "Don't worry about it. It's their house, they were just seeing who was here. No harm done."

He kissed my cheek and instructed, "Come inside. And please relax. We aren't at work."

The gravel crunched beneath our feet as we walked up to the house, Jason taking my hand and Tony walking a few steps ahead. "Interesting names," I said as we reached the front door.

Tony laughed. "Lurch was very lanky as a pup, so he earned the name."

"And Sonny?" I asked.

Jason laughed. "You saw how he collapsed?"

I gave him a side glance as Tony explained, "Jay always thought it was hilarious how huge he was, yet when the prospect of attention was on the cards he hit the deck."

"He goes down like a sack of shit, he means," Jase chipped in as Tony pushed open the front door.

"Go through to the bar," Tony said as we stepped inside. "I'm going to go and lock the pair of them up."

"Oh, no don't," I protested, "it isn't their fault."

"No, no. I usually keep them in the courtyard when I have company. They're much too large to be climbing on people. Get yourselves a drink, I won't be long."

Jason led me into a games room off to the left, housing a pool table, juke box, and a couple of sofas, and in the corner was a hand carved bar. The floor was solid oak, giving the place a cottagey feel despite the size of the rooms. Jason smiled and asked, "Prosecco?"

I shrugged. "If he has any."

He tipped his head to the side, and I followed him. Behind the bar were four glass-fronted fridges displaying mostly beers, ciders, wines, and mixers. He patted the bar and said, "The spirits are under here."

I smiled. "Oh, not spirits. I'm happy with prosecco. Thanks."

"Sit down, I'll bring it over."

He opened the bottle as I made for the sofas, pausing when I noticed the large canvas print on the wall behind the largest couch.

"My goddaughter, Poppy," Tony explained. I jumped, not realizing he was there until he spoke.

"Sorry, I tend not to wear shoes."

"Meaning he's a creeping bloody Jesus," Jase teased, handing me a flute of prosecco and flopping down on the sofa.

"She's stunning," I said, looking up at Tony.

He gestured for me to sit down. "That was taken years ago. I should get an updated one, really. I don't see nearly enough of her since I live up here."

I sat next to Jase, and he put his hand on my knee. "You live here on your own?"

Tony laughed. "For now."

"He keeps telling me he'll work on it, but he never does. Too wrapped up in work, aren't you, mate?"

Tony rolled his eyes. "Someone has to build the empire."

Jase held up his hands, "Hey, I brought the product. Selling it wasn't my job, we agreed on that."

"Cara agreed on that," Tony argued pointedly. "Did you open me a beer?"

"No. I didn't know if you wanted that horrible grape juice you like or what. I'll have a coke."

Tony turned and got drinks while I looked around the room.

"What's up?" Jason asked quietly.

"Nothing. It's just weird, you're my bosses."

He laughed and kissed my cheek. "Not today we're not. Relax. He's my best mate. I want you to get to know him. I already know Haylie."

Tony retrieved Jason's can of coke and tossed it in his direction, and Jason had to act quickly to catch it. Laughing at his expression, he sat on the opposite sofa and said, "Please relax, Nathalie."

"It's... it's just Nat," I insisted, trying to sound chilled.

Tony wasn't buying it. "Honestly, Nat, I don't like the formality at work. Please, don't let it follow me here. I'd drop it there entirely if it weren't for one or two staff members who would take advantage."

"Really?" Jason enquired, apparently surprised. "Who?"

"Chantal," I answered without thinking.

Tony laughed. "How is training that one going?"

I took a drink. "It isn't. She'll get it eventually, but she isn't picking it up as quickly as I'd hoped. It's okay, I'll get her there." I sat back as they looked at each other, some silent conversation going on I wasn't privy to and I added, "Anyway, I don't really want to talk shop." I tilted my head and looked at Tony. "It looks like an unlikely pairing, tell me, how did you two become friends?"

"I told you, we shared a house," Jason said, putting his drink on the table in front of us.

"That's what you told her?" Tony queried, arching a brow. "We found ourselves in the same building. I refused to go into halls, wanting a more authentic uni experience. I didn't expect to end up with this reprobate."

I looked at Jase. "Reprobate? Him?"

Tony snorted. "My idea of a wild night was tame compared to what he introduced me to. Rich was somewhere between the two of us. Cara... Well, she picked up much of the mess."

"You introduced them to depth charges, didn't you?" I gasped with disbelief.

Jase shrugged. "It was fun. Rich is from the valleys, Tony was a straight-laced rich boy, they needed help."

I shook my head. "Poor Cara."

"She got her own back many times over," Tony reminisced fondly. He was interrupted by the dogs barking, and Jase got up.

"I'll get it."

I looked at him with my brows drawn in.

"Food," he said as an explanation, heading for the door.

"I didn't tell you what I wanted..."

"Jay doesn't do small orders," Tony explained as Jase left us. "He'll have ordered before you even left. I can guarantee there's something you like."

"That's just a waste."

Tony shrugged. "It's his thing. We all have our thing. I'll feed leftovers to the boys."

I looked at him. "Do we?"

"Of course," he responded brightly. "I'm known to do things to excess myself."

I drained my glass, and Tony got up to retrieve the bottle from the bar. The front door closed, and I looked up to see Jase coming back with a stack of pizza boxes.

"Help yourself."

I chewed the inside of my cheek.

"If all you want is one slice, just take the one slice."

"He does this to you often, then?" I asked, taking some from the nearest box. It felt odd eating from a pizza box on the sofa in that crazy huge house, but the two of them seemed perfectly relaxed so I followed suit.

"At least once every six weeks," Tony answered, examining his own box. "I tried to resist years ago, but honestly it's easier to indulge him."

I took a breath. "Noted."

Jase rubbed his foot against mine and I smiled to myself.

*  *  *

After we'd eaten, Tony took the boxes away and Jason poured me another drink.

"Aren't you having one? We could get a taxi home," I suggested when he opened a second can of coke.

"I don't want to drink. Not tonight."

I frowned at him and put my glass down. "Why?"

"Because I don't need a drink tonight," he answered, and I couldn't question him further because Tony came back.

I was uncomfortably full, so much so my third glass of prosecco was looking like a challenge, so I took a small sip and put it back on the table then commented, "I can't believe he managed to corrupt you."

"I wasn't all bad," Jase protested while Tony laughed.

"It's true," he agreed. "He did have a positive influence here and there. In our second year, he talked Cara into taking a part-time job. Since Jay was already working in that awful drive-through place, she talked me into applying too. Worst two years of my life."

Jase held up a finger and interjected, "I told you to come with me, but you were above flipping burgers."

"Yes. Well, the ignorance of youth. Suffice to say my eyes were opened and when we began taking on staff, I vowed never to treat them the way we were treated in that hellhole. It's the one rule we stick to throughout the company and will always be our ethos."

"Where did you work?" I asked, intrigued.

"Telecommunications call center," he grumbled bitterly. "Never again. Ever."

"I suppose the prospect of going back to that made you more driven."

"And some," he said, finishing his bottle. "I swore never to raise my voice, lose my temper, or blame a staff member for what they couldn't control. So far, I think it's gone well. What did you do with yourself between leaving school and walking through our doors?"

Jason sat straighter at my side and put my hand on his leg. When he sat back, I responded, "Well, I went to college to do an admin course, connected with someone we went to school with, got married, got divorced, earned a degree and lost my mind working in payroll for a massive, soulless company and hated every minute of it. I've kept one close friend all my life. She's a bit mad, but I wouldn't change her for the world. I haven't had a very interesting life, but Haylie keeps it colorful." I looked at him thoughtfully for a moment, then added, "I think she'd scare you half to death if I'm honest. I'll have to introduce you."

He grinned. "I'll hold you to that. We could all do with more color."

Jason stepped in and expertly steered the conversation in another direction by asking Tony how his gym was coming together. It wasn't necessary, but I was grateful, and I listened as they discussed the advantages and disadvantages of different pieces of exercise equipment I either hadn't heard of or knew I hated to use.

The sun was setting when Jason suggested we get home.

Tony took my hand and helped me up from the sofa. "Thank you for coming, Nat. I've enjoyed getting to know the real you."

"And you. Thanks for having us, it's been lovely."

"We'll do it again in a few weeks, yeah?" Jase suggested, taking my other hand.

"I'm usually around," Tony replied cheerfully.

He didn't see us out, clearing away my half full glass, and the empty cans and bottles he and Jason had used. When the front door closed behind us, I looked to Jason and smiled.

"That was nice."

"I didn't think he'd start asking awkward questions," he said at once, taking my hand again and making for the car.

"Can't always avoid it," I noted, trying to make him feel better. "It's fine, don't worry about it."

He opened my door for me and let me get in. "Still, I'm sorry."

I fastened my seatbelt and sat in the silence of his car while he made his way to the driver's side, and took a deep breath. It was uncomfortable being asked, but I couldn't keep hiding it.

"It happened," I reiterated when he closed his door. "A lot of things happened, and we've moved on. I can't hide from it forever, and it isn't so bad talking about it. Not now."

He leaned over and kissed me before starting the car. The engine roared, and I startled.

"Sorry. I keep forgetting."

"Forgetting what?"

He raised his brows and looked at me. "You know what. I'll try harder to remember."

I half smiled, grateful he considered it, and looked down at my lap. "Thank you."

The car began to move and he turned on the radio. "Anything for you. Now let's get you home, I want my dessert."

## CHAPTER NINETEEN

Guiding me back onto the bed, his lips trailed down my chest, between my breasts and then were gone. I couldn't see, a silk scarf was tied around my eyes, blocking out all the light in the room. But the lights were on.

"Okay?"

I swallowed. "I think so." I couldn't manage anything more than a whisper.

He pulled back, and I caught the back of his neck with my hand. "Don't—"

"'Think so' isn't good enough. I'm not pushing this on you, babe."

His hand tugged at the scarf and I grabbed his wrist. "No... I'm okay. Really, I'm okay."

"Tell me if you're not," he reminded me, and I relaxed as he kissed me again.

I nodded, and his mouth left mine.

There was nothing for several moments, and I began to feel uneasy. But not in a bad way. He was watching me. He hadn't left the bed, but he wasn't touching me at all. I closed my eyes, despite the scarf blindfolding me, and licked my lips. Waiting.

Something soft brushed my neck, and I released the breath I'd just taken with a relieved sigh. My cheeks heated, the prickle of warmth spreading down my neck to my chest. The soft thing followed, slowly, tickling its way over my exposed and sensitive skin. That was when I worked out that it was the Ostrich feather.

"I wish you could see this," he whispered in my ear.

The sudden sound startled me, but more importantly it sent a wave of tingles from the back of my head and down to my shoulders. I wanted to ask what, but the item brushing my skin was moving on, down to my right breast and around the areola.

I raised a hand, and he stopped the movement. "Ah-ah…" he chastised.

I pressed my lips together and lowered my hand. He returned the feather to my neck and began again. By the time he reached my breasts, my nipples were erect and straining to be touched. My back arched, and he took the feather away.

I groaned, lifting a hand, reaching for him, and the bed moved.

He was only gone for a few moments, returning and brushing something cold and smooth over my thigh. "Give me your hand," he demanded, and I heard the crackle of Velcro as he tested the satin at my thigh to make sure it wasn't too tight. My wrist was secured to my thigh, and he did the same on the other side, placing my legs together and leaving me on my back. "No wriggling."

This time he started at my feet, but the item he tickled me with had changed. This was firmer, but still soft. A different kind of soft. It trailed from the top of my foot to my thigh, my skin prickling as it skimmed over the contours of my muscles, and when it brushed the back of my hand, a wave of tickles spread up my arm. He didn't follow, instead brushing over my tummy, letting the fronds of whatever he held skim over my skin and up over my breasts.

A sharp intake of breath broke the silence of the room, my reaction to my nipples feeling the friction of his object of choice.

"Suede," he whispered, laying it against my skin, splaying it over my chest and leaving it there.

Something cold brushed my left nipple, then my right. Metal. There was a click and a low hum as the item began to vibrate against the erect nub. The vibrations traveled across my skin, spreading out from the epicenter of my nipple and down. He followed as though he knew, the cold tip of the tiny steel vibrator marking its path to my navel. He avoided the scars there, taking it down the other side so I could fully feel everything he did, and to the apex of my thighs. I squirmed, tugging my wrists up, but they were secured. His hand stayed, the vibrator leaving my skin, and I stilled.

I held my breath, waiting, visualizing where I needed him to go, what I needed him to do, but he didn't move for what felt like minutes. I listened. I waited. I was about to speak when the hum of the vibrator stopped, and he placed his hand on my thigh.

With the gentlest of touches he parted my legs, and I remained as still as I could manage as the anticipation built. I silently begged him to touch me again, to reach down and feel how wet I was for him. How much I needed him.

"I can see how wet you are."

I would have felt ashamed before, hearing him utter those words, but I couldn't seem to muster those feelings. There was awe and desire in his voice. Satisfaction. This was what he needed. This was his goal, and I was giving him exactly what he craved. The torture of waiting, of enduring the process to get what I needed was entirely worth it.

He kissed me like he was starved. With my hands firmly attached to my thighs, all I could do was kiss him back, but the urge to reach for him was killing me. "I need to touch you."

He kissed down my neck and mumbled into the hollow at the base, "Not yet."

I dug my nails into my palms and gasped as his tongue ran over my nipple. It was almost painful as it brushed over the erect, sensitive nub, causing fire to spread over my skin. Unable to move my hands, I pushed back my shoulders, digging my heels into the mattress. I was so absorbed in what I was feeling, I didn't feel him move his hand. I didn't expect the feel of the soft silicone, but the relief I felt as he pressed the soft vibrations against my clit made me sob.

He moved the tip in slow, gentle circles, and I parted my legs further, desperate to feel everything, angling my hips in the hope of feeling more. I was close, and when I bucked my hips and the pressure increased for a second, I was sure I was going to come, but he was watching me closely and knew just when to stop. The absence was agony. My body was screaming for more, but he'd withdrawn completely. I lay still, panting, my clit throbbing and an orgasm building, desperate for release.

It all happened at once. His mouth closed over my clit and the vibrator slid inside, and the blood in my veins sang for him as the orgasm he'd built flowed freely. My body convulsed, my internal muscles clutching at the synthetic phallus that continued to send wracking waves of tingles racing through me. The way he sucked at my clit, the feel of his tongue massaging the tight, erect nub, brought me crashing down and spiralling up in a matter of seconds.

Taking his mouth away, he increased the movements of the vibrator. With my head tilted back and my hips rotating, he fucked another orgasm from me so intense, my head throbbed. It was better knowing he was watching. That he'd gotten me there. That he saw my face and watched every muscle in my body go taut.

He was still fucking me when he removed the scarf. His eyes held mine as I came again, then in a smooth movement, he withdrew the vibrator and slid into me, unfastening the cuffs as he did.

I reached for his face, pushing my fingers into his hair and kissing him as he ground his hips into mine. The feel of him, and not the toy he'd been using, was incredible. I don't know why. Maybe it was because it was all of him, but it was something the dildo couldn't replicate.

His fingers tangled in my hair and he kissed me fiercely before pushing away, withdrawing as he went.

"Touch yourself."

It wasn't like him to be so demanding, and it took me by surprise. "Wh—"

He took my hand, guiding it to my pussy, reaching for his cock with the other. He began stroking, my fingers began moving, and soon I found a rhythm that matched his.

His eyes fixed on my hand, and he growled, "You're fucking perfect."

And that was my undoing. I couldn't speak, riding the crest of another orgasm, but I watched him, watching me, as I came. He was right there with me, ropes of come pumping from him, spreading over my stomach and thighs. And he never looked away, holding my gaze as he reached his climax, proving it was all for me. I got him there as he'd done the same for me.

Breathing heavily, I closed my eyes and smiled. He landed beside me, his arms wrapping around me, pulling me close. "I mean it. You're the most perfect thing I've ever seen."

I pressed my lips together and smiled, lowering my head into his chest. "I love you."

"You have no idea."

I was sure it was the other way around, but I wouldn't argue. Right then, everything was as it should be. I didn't need to say anything else.

## CHAPTER TWENTY

We woke late. Still, I was up first, despite being the one who'd had a few glasses of wine. I looked at the state of my bed and couldn't see the duvet. The feather was by my feet, alongside a very cruel looking whip thing. It had so many tails on it, I wondered why the hell he'd brought that near me, and then remembered the suede. A small silver vibrator, no bigger than my finger, was at the top of the bed by my pillow. I couldn't see the large silicone one anywhere. Knowing they'd need a thorough cleaning, I tried to get off the bed without waking him and failed.

"Are you running off again?"

"You dare?" I challenged, laughing and swinging my feet out. That was when I found the big one, on the floor. I didn't remember hearing it fall off. "No. I'm going to the loo and getting these cleaned up."

He stretched, yawned, then looked at me. "Leave them and come here."

I dodged his grasp. "Five minutes."

He followed me into the bathroom. I sat down anyway, I was absolutely bursting, while he took his toothbrush from the side and cleaned his teeth.

"You said we were staying in bed," I said, flushing the toilet and washing my hands before reaching for my own brush.

"Oh, we are," he verified, looking me up and down, then putting his brush in the holder. I brushed my teeth as he stepped behind me and grasped me around the waist. He rested his chin on my shoulder and kissed my neck. "You were amazing last night."

I carried on brushing my teeth, trying so damn hard not to blush. I failed.

"Do you want to go back to bed, or shall we go out for breakfast, and then go back to bed?"

I wanted to go back to bed, but I was also hungry. "Well, I could eat…" I mumbled through a mouth full of foam.

He chuckled next to my ear, and my body responded with a wave of tingles running down my back. "Steady on," he said, feeling my skin prickle. "I'll handle that once you're fed. First, shower."

He turned on the water and watched me brush. I left him in privacy so I could go and get ready.

\* \* \*

We both got ready in record time, and I was just locking the door when he called, "Change of plan, we'll have to take your car."

"Why?" I asked, walking to the end of the drive.

"Some fucker slashed my tires."

He didn't sound too bothered by it. Almost as though he expected it. I was horrified. "I told you to park on the drive."

He shrugged. "I'll call someone out to sort it while we have breakfast. Come on, you can show off your tiny car."

I watched him walk back up the drive to my car frowning. It wasn't usual for things like that to happen, not on my quiet little street. The neighbors were a pain in the arse for parking their cars badly, but they certainly wouldn't vandalize someone else's.

\* \* \*

It was getting late by the time we arrived in town, and I parked in a small private car park just over the road from a small pancake house he said he liked. His phone chimed, and without bothering to look at it he added, "I need to make a phone call, work. Can you go in and order drinks? I'll follow you in a couple of minutes."

Leaning over to kiss him, I unbuckled my belt and smiled, dropping my keys in his lap. "Anything in particular?"

He was already looking at his phone. "Just coffee, thanks."

I walked into the little café, wondering why he was working on a Saturday and went directly to the counter. I was waiting for someone to take my order when I heard a familiar voice, and looked over to see Sandra sitting with two other women at the table behind me. She noticed me and scowled.

Turning back to the counter, I froze, wondering if she was going to say something. I considered warning her that Jase was with me, since she was off work—apparently sick—and was about to turn and go to her table, when she came up behind me. "Enjoying my job, Nathalie?" she hissed in my ear.

I didn't know what to say. Obviously one of the other girls had contacted her and told her I'd swooped in and took her job. I wanted to set the record straight, but didn't know how to handle that level of confrontation. "I... Tony... I..." I stuttered.

I was panicking. I wanted to explain I was backed into a corner over it. That I didn't want it. But when I turned to face her and saw the look in her eye, I lost my nerve completely. I was saved by the waitress who waited at the counter for me to place our order. "Two coffees, please."

She walked away, busying herself with the coffee machine, and Sandra stepped closer to me.

"Didn't take you long, did it?"

My stomach clenched with anxiety. While I wasn't really one for confrontation, it wasn't what she was saying to me that upset me, I didn't give a shit what she thought, not really. It was that this would make my work life difficult and, more urgently, how she stood behind me and said it quietly. The way *he* used to.

My instinct was to escape. But I was trapped between her and the counter. Thankfully, she was interrupted as our drinks were put down in front of me. I forced a smile and handed over the money to pay for them, with Sandra still at my back, then turned to face her. "Tony asked me to temp it rather than get someone new in."

"I heard different. I heard you were sleeping your way to the top, and my job was a performance bonus. I wonder how that's going down with—"

"Hello Sandra, you're looking remarkably well."

My heart stopped for all the right reasons. I'd never felt so relieved to hear someone's voice.

Sandra's face slackened. "Jay…"

I looked up at him, but rather than feel relieved he was here, I tensed. His stance was aggressive. Protective.

"Mr. Locksley," he corrected, his voice as cold as the glint in his eye.

"I was just saying how nice it was to see—" she spluttered, trying to backtrack.

He stepped back, making sure to be well out of touching distance, and said in a low voice, "Nathalie's position at the company is none of your business. My life, in or outside of the company, is none of your damn business."

I watched her, wondering what she was going to do next. The answer was nothing. She seemed to freeze.

Jason stepped closer to my side, his hand brushing mine as he asked, "Are those our drinks, Nat?"

I nodded, unable to look away from Sandra. The color had drained from her face, and she looked like she was caught between screaming an obscenity and bursting into tears.

He picked up both saucers and faced her again. I glanced his way to see him looking at her heels. "Your sick note is due next Friday. Make it a long one," he ordered, before turning and picking up both our drinks and moving away from the bar. I followed him to a table at the other end of the cafe, trying not to glance back over my shoulder to see what her friends were doing.

"Sciatica..." Jase said with a sniff. "In those shoes?"

I couldn't muster a smile. "They've been talking..."

He sipped his coffee. "And?"

"And they think I'm—"

"They can think what they like."

"That's easy for you to say, you're not around."

He looked wounded. I wasn't sure why, but I scrambled to rephrase. "What I mean is—"

"I know what you mean, and honestly, I'll replace the lot of them if they keep this shit up. It's none of their fucking business. They aren't paid to poke their noses into our private lives."

"She's management." It was a weak argument, but I knew he couldn't just fire her.

"She's went four weeks beyond her probationary period and thrown in a long-term sick note. She's sitting in here with her friends, having a ball, while we pay her a full fucking salary, you're doing the job she should be doing, better than she ever did I might add, and she thinks she can have a pop at you?"

Uncomfortable to the point of nausea, I kept my eyes on him. He was looking over at her as he spoke to me, making me edgier. I didn't dare look around to see what was happening, but his attention was firmly fixed on her table. "I just don't want any friction at work..."

He finally looked at me, and his expression changed. I don't know what he saw, I was too anxious to assess myself, but I saw his brow furrow, and he lowered his head.

"Sorry. I heard how she spoke to you, and I don't ever want to see you treated like... Well, nobody speaks to you like that. Nobody."

While his voice was calm, there was a fierceness to it. I didn't remember being defended like this by anyone but Haylie. I wasn't sure how I felt about it. "You can't threaten her like that though. I mean, it doesn't look good, does it?"

The scraping of chairs and the click of heels on the tile floor drew his attention back to her table. "I don't give a fuck how it looks. She'll stick in another sick note and when that runs out, she's fired."

I was mortified. "She has rent to pay…"

"I have a business to run."

I looked down at my hands and picked at my nails. His hands closed around them, thumbs brushing over mine, and he murmured, "I'm sorry. I'm trying not to. I don't usually get angry, really, but when it comes to you my back gets right up. I can't stop it."

"You don't have to protect me, Jase."

He raised my hands to his lips and kissed them. "I do. I will."

"I'm hungry."

It was a lie, but I needed the subject changed.

He nodded at something behind me. "Let her get her arse out the door, and I'll order you the biggest stack of pancakes and bacon you've seen in your life."

I smiled, dipping my chin. He watched me intently for a few moments, and I began to feel self-conscious. "What?"

"I like looking at you."

I laughed. "Why?"

"Because you're beautiful, and I don't get to look at you enough. What?"

I shook my head.

"Don't? Why?" he asks in response.

I shrugged.

He grinned at me. "Get used to it, babe. It's not stopping."

I shook my head and sat back, forcing him to release my hands. "Get me some breakfast."

He gave me a small salute and got up, leaning over to kiss me before heading to the counter. Left alone, I thought back to his car. When he came back I said, "When are you getting the car sorted?"

"It's being towed now. Tony's seeing to it, he knows a guy."

I nodded. "I'm so sorry. I didn't think that would happen. Not on my street. It's usually so quiet."

"It's not the first time. Don't worry, it's expected with a car like that."

I frowned at him. "That's not right, though, is it?"

"It is what it is. Don't worry about it."

But I did. He didn't understand just how unusual it was for that to happen. Everyone looked out for everyone else on my street. It was a real little community. I left it, but I was determined to ask around as soon as he departed, and see if anyone had seen anything.

## CHAPTER TWENTY-ONE

The month passed in the usual way, except I didn't see quite as much of Haylie. I didn't pry, assuming they'd returned to their previous bliss, and saved some money by not going out. Instead, I busied myself with decorating the living room, putting the saved money to better use. The final weekend of October arrived, and Jason with it. I'd left my car on the road, leaving the drive empty for his car. I heard him pull in and looked out of the window, surprised to see a black Audi A7 in place of his white i8. Not only was it a considerably cheaper car, it wasn't as sporty.

"Where's your car?" I asked, opening the front door.

He kissed me, smiled, and teased, "I've missed you too."

"Sorry, I just wasn't expecting to see... Never mind."

He looked at me for a second then cupped my cheek in his hand. "Do me a favor."

"What's that?" I queried, leaning into his hand and closing my eyes.

"Go and get ready, we have to be at the races at eight."

"What? You can't drop that on me short notice. I haven't had my hair done," I argued, glaring at him.

"It doesn't need doing. You're fine, just go and get ready to go out like we're going for dinner."

I didn't think he understood just how much effort I put into getting ready when he was due to visit. Thankfully, most of it was already done, I just didn't have my hair styled or a face full of makeup because we weren't supposed to be going out.

"What are you wearing?" I asked, looking him up and down. He couldn't go in jeans.

"My suit is in the car. I'll take considerably less time to get ready than you will."

"I don't believe this," I grumbled, turning and heading up the stairs. "Why the short notice?"

"I'll tell you in a minute," he called out, then the front door closed.

I went into the bedroom and started dragging hair styling paraphernalia out of the wardrobe while listening for him coming back. He was only a couple of minutes, and by the time my straighteners had heated up he was climbing the stairs. "The room looks nice. What brought that on?"

"Boredom. Why do we have to go to the races tonight?"

He threw his suit onto the bed and dropped a pair of polished shoes on the floor at the bedside. "I was invited. Looks like we're being weighed up against the competition. It's common practice, schmoozing."

"Why can't Tony go?"

"For the same reason you don't want to, I imagine," he speculated with a look of amusement. Then he moved across the room and bent over me, leaning his chin on my shoulder. "You can feign a headache at nine thirty and spare us if you like."

"I have a headache now," I claimed with just a touch of self-pity. "I don't like stuff dropped on me. You could have said this morning."

"I didn't know this morning, Tony dropped this on me as I was driving up here."

I looked at him through the mirror with my brows raised. "Yeah? Where's the suit from then?"

"The office. I keep one up here and one at the other office. Good practice should I have an emergency schmooze to attend and no time to go home."

I narrowed my eyes at him. "Fine. Did you shower?"

He grinned at me through the mirror and kissed my cheek. "I'll go now."

I took a deep breath and got on with making myself look presentable.

* * *

"Turn it off."

"I can't turn off the sun, babe."

"God… What time is it?" I groaned into my pillow as his arm circled my waist.

"Eleven. You had a good night."

I had. It turned out the guy he was meeting had a private box or had hired one from someone for the purpose of impressing Jase. The latter seemed much more likely. That meant we had a private bar, tote facilities, and a full hot buffet laid out for the evening. I'd taken full advantage and was paying for it.

"Oh, god. Did I embarrass you?"

He laughed. "Not at all. He was quite taken with you."

I remembered. Jason had introduced me as the Admin Manager of the local branch and his girlfriend when we arrived, and I was treated as though my opinion was as important as his. "Yeah. Oh, my head…"

"I'll get you some painkillers. Just give me five," he said, rolling out of bed. "Are they still in the drawer?"

I nodded and watched him go when his phone started to ring. "Jase, phone!" I called after him, and he came back to grab it. "All right, mate? Yeah, not bad." He conversed, moving back out of the bedroom and into the bathroom, where he rummaged in the drawer. He was still talking when he came back into the bedroom. "No, we separated. Yeah, yeah, I'll ask her. I'm sure she'd love to. No, I'm sorry. Yeah, we'll be there. Thanks for checking in, sorry about… No. Okay. Yeah."

I rolled onto my back. "What?"

He put his phone down on my bedside table, and passed me the painkillers and a glass of water.

"Wedding invitation. The ex must have received it, and didn't tell me or bother to RSVP. That was the groom checking final numbers."

I took the pills and washed them down with the full glass of water before flopping back onto the bed. "And you're going with her?"

He snorted. "No, I'm taking you."

"Really?" It came out as a croak. I was not well.

He climbed back into bed and held me. "Who else would I take?"

I shrugged. "Dunno."

"Nat, I understand why you thought I was going to disappear earlier on, but why do you think it now? It's been months. I love you. I'm not going anywhere."

I shrugged again. The truth was, I was expecting it to fall apart. I was just waiting for it to go to hell. There was no way I could be as happy as I was without something terrible happening. I was sure I could feel it creeping up.

"Look at me."

I glanced up, my eyes meeting his.

"I love you. This isn't a fling for me, believe me. I'm in this for the long haul. I know it's all a bit mad, but I'm working on getting some things sorted so you can come down to me occasionally. I just need some time. While this is what I want, it surprised me a bit."

I swallowed and nodded my head, tears welling in my eyes.

"What's wrong? What did I say?"

He sounded so worried I laughed. "Nothing."

"Then why are you crying?"

I buried my face in his chest. "I'm happy."

He kissed the top of my head as he held me close, and I wrapped my arm around his waist, savoring the feeling of being safe in his arms. Of being loved. Of being all he needed.

\* \* \*

I fell asleep and woke up to find Jason gone. I was feeling much better, but I was hungry, and I moved to get out of bed. "Jase?"

There was no answer, so I took myself to the bathroom and started the process of getting dressed.

Back in the bedroom, I heard a car pull into the drive and tugged a shirt over my head as my phone beeped. At least I thought it was mine, until I sat on the edge of the bed, picked it up, and read the message on the screen.

*It's date night tomorrow. I can't wait. I've missed you so much x*

"Babe? Are you up?" he called as the front door closed.

My blood ran cold. He'd done it to me again. No, this was worse. He hadn't left me, or her. He was stringing us both along. Every hope I dared to have shattered with the sound of his voice.

He'd been lying to me for months.

After promising me. He'd made me believe he wouldn't hurt me and lied about his entire life.

The tables had turned. I was the other woman.

I'd given him everything. I shared the darkest moments of my life with him that I hadn't shared with anyone but Haylie, and he'd lied and cheated his way back into my life, stringing me along, telling me he was divorced.

And Tony was in on it.

I put the phone down where I found it and answered, "Yeah. Where have you been?"

He ran up the stairs and appeared at the door, holding up a paper bag in one hand and two milkshakes in the other. "I went out for burgers. Not good for us, but they will help your hangover. Back in bed."

I didn't move.

"What's up?"

"I thought it was mine... I thought it was you..."

He followed my gaze to the table. To his phone.

The look on his face was one of alarm. "Who called?"

I shook my head. "Nobody. Just a message. I read it thinking..." I choked back the tears stinging my eyes. I couldn't do it. I couldn't sit there and explain myself. I needed him away from me. Trying to remain calm, I pleaded, "I'm sorry… Jase, I need you to go."

"No, wait. Just…" He reached for the phone and read the text on the screen. Despite my reaction, he looked relieved. He even smiled. Then he said, "Fuck… Right, I can explain."

"Can you?" I asked with a humorless laugh, getting to my feet. "Does she mean nothing to you? Is it not what it looks like?"

He stepped aside and let me by, then followed me down the stairs. "None of that. Listen—"

"No. You fucking lied to me. It's her, isn't it? Your wife?"

I rushed through the living room and into the kitchen, looking for my bag. He followed, dumping the takeout bag on the counter. I flinched at the sound of the paper rustling. He didn't notice. "Nathalie, she isn't my wife. She's my daughter."

Nausea turned my stomach, and I closed my eyes for a second, trying to calm myself down. Certain I was going to be sick, I put my hand over my mouth.

"I wanted to tell you, but when you said what you did—"

"When did I ever mention kids?" I snapped.

"You said you didn't have any of that baggage. I thought you meant you didn't *like* them, so I didn't mention Poppy because she has nothing to do with this."

Poppy. The image of the beautiful child from Tony's games room flashed in my mind. "Oh, for…" And then it dawned on me. The little girl looked a lot like Jason around the eyes, but her nose and mouth? They belonged to someone else I knew.

A family company, indeed. How could I have been so stupid?

"It's Cara? Cara is your ex-wife?"

"For fuck's sake, Nat." His voice raised with exasperation and my stomach turned.

"You aren't divorced, are you?"

He bowed his head. That was when I decided I had to leave and made for the door, but the bile I was choking down rose, and I had to turn and lean over the sink instead.

I let it come, turning on the tap to wash my vomit away and shrugging his hand off when he touched my shoulder.

"Nathalie, please, hear me out. Let me explain."

Cupping my hand to catch the cold water, I rinsed my mouth then turned away, leaving the tap running, and moved back into the living room. He followed, and I turned around with my hand up. He stopped in his tracks. "Explain what? The family you keep in another town? Fucking hell, I'm the other woman, aren't I? I'm wrecking the home of the woman who gave me the best job I've ever had. Shit, you don't do this stuff by halves, do you Jason?"

He looked genuinely wounded but didn't try to speak again. He just looked at me. It wasn't working. I wasn't listening to any more of his lies. "Do not be here when I get back. Get your shit and get out. I mean it, Jase. If you come near me again, I'll… I'll phone the police."

I didn't hear his response, the door slammed behind me, and I was down the drive without a backward glance. He didn't follow me out. I glanced at the house as I drove by, getting one last look at his car, at the home I'd been planning on asking him to share with me. There were no tears. I was too angry to cry. Just a lump in my throat, and the weight of disappointment crushing my chest.

It had been too good to be true, the little voice in my head gloated. There was no way that was ever going to last.

## CHAPTER TWENTY-TWO

*I* let myself into the office the following morning and got everything set up before Tony arrived. When I heard the door open, I went straight into the staff room and put the kettle on, keeping to my usual routine. I was still an employee here, for the time being, and I wasn't planning to give any of them a reason to end my contract on bad terms, however messy it had ended up.

"Nathalie…"

I swallowed the lump in my throat and carried on with what I was doing. He didn't leave, so I said, "It's just Nat."

"I didn't expect you to come in today," he admitted. There was a hint of apology in his tone. "If you need to take the day off, I understand."

"Thank you, Tony, but I'm okay," I stated, turning and handing him his mug.

I was not okay.

His expression told me I was doing a terrible job of hiding it. I knew my face was blotchy, my skin was pale, and I looked like I hadn't slept in three days, but I wouldn't be taking a personal day over something as stupid as this.

"Honestly, it was just a shock, that's all. I'm fine."

"So, you'll let him explain?"

"Fuck no." It was out of my mouth before I had chance to stop it. Thankfully, Tony didn't look offended. "What I mean is, he had enough opportunities to speak to me about his wife and daughter. You were more forthcoming about his child than he was."

He looked at me with a small, apologetic frown.

"Tony, I'm sorry… I didn't want to mix it up for this reason. I knew this would happen."

He shook his head. "You did nothing… For what it's worth, he and Cara have been separated for years. They kept up the façade for Poppy, but there hasn't been a relationship for quite some time. They co-parent. They work together. They're still on friendly terms because they must be. I did urge him to mention Poppy, but he couldn't seem to find the right time."

I didn't say anything, but he seemed to know what I was thinking and explained, "Poppy is nine. She's a bright, friendly, sociable girl, if a little coddled. Jay has taken her to the cinema and out for dinner most Sundays since he and Cara split. It's their date night. I know how it appeared, Nat. But honestly, in the thirteen years I've known him, he hasn't looked at anyone the way he looks at you."

I turned and picked up my mug. "I'm sorry, Tony, but I have a lot to do today. Excuse me."

He bowed his head and let me leave without another word. It wasn't his fault his friend had screwed me over again, but I couldn't stand here and accept his apologies on Jason's behalf.

It was a long morning. Chantal didn't seem to be listening to a damn word I said, and when lunch time arrived, I decided to just sit in my car with a mug of coffee and collect my thoughts.

My phone rang, and I ignored it.

My phone beeped, and I ignored it.

I received an email, and I ignored it.

When the phone rang again I picked it up and watched the screen until it stopped. Then I blocked his number and deleted my social media apps. I didn't bother to listen to the voicemail he left, and instead dialed Haylie's number, bursting into tears the moment she answered.

* * *

I returned from the bar with a tray loaded with full shot glasses and a bottle of prosecco.

"How long have you been here? You look like shit. What the fuck is going on?" she questioned, picking up a shot glass and downing the tequila.

I hadn't bothered with salt and lime, they weren't there to be enjoyed, and downed one myself. "Two hours," I replied, nodding to the ice bucket with an empty bottle upturned inside. "I drank a bottle before you got here. The bastard fucked me over."

"How?" she asked, taking another glass.

"Wife. Kid. Still lives with them." I downed one.

Her brows rose, and she flopped back in her seat. "Well… Shit. How did you find out?"

I looked at the four remaining glasses and picked up another. "His kid sent him a message about date night on Sunday. I read it by accident, jumping to the usual conclusion at talk of a date night." I downed the drink.

"And he said…?"

"That he could explain."

"And did you let him?"

I downed another. "No. I threw up and drove off, in that order."

"Well you seem to know enough about it now," she concluded calmly. "Who told you?"

"Tony, mainly." I reached for the last shot.

She slapped my hand away. "No more of that shit for you, you can't handle it. And what did Tony say?"

I scowled at her, picked up the prosecco, and filled my glass instead. "That he's been separated from Cara for years, that Poppy is a nice kid, and he takes her on a date every Sunday."

"Cara who interviewed you?" she asked, taking the prosecco and drinking from the bottle.

I cringed. "Yeah. Her."

She was about to say something when my phone rang. Knowing I'd blocked his number I answered it without looking.

"Nathalie, please don't hang up."

My stomach hollowed out, and I was sure I turned several shades paler. "I'm not doing this, Jase. I can't. You knew… I… I told you…" I choked back the tears, fighting to keep myself together long enough to finish what I needed to say. "Stop calling me. Please, just let me walk away from this with a shred of dignity."

"If that's what you really want. Just know that I'm sorry, babe. I… Well, it doesn't matter now, but I'm sorry."

I turned it off and let it drop onto the table. Haylie shifted to sit next to me and pulled me into her arms as the tears fell. "I'm so sorry, Nat."

I sobbed into her shoulder until I had no tears left to shed. Drained, exhausted, and heartbroken, I finished my drink in silence and stared down at the table.

"I've told Tommo I'm staying with you tonight," she murmured, stroking my hair. "Shall we get you home?"

I shook my head. "No. You go home. I'll be okay."

She laughed. "Yeah, course you will. Come on, tipsy."

She picked up my phone and shoved it in my bag, before shouldering it and dragging me to my feet.

I let her lead me out and bundle me into a taxi.

"What about you and Tommo?" I enquired when the car set off moving.

"We're fine," she answered, nudging me. "We're perfect."

"Are you going to elaborate?"

"No. I'm going to get you some toast and into bed, so you don't have to call in sick at work tomorrow."

I groaned. "Oh, god…"

She snorted. I didn't think she was funny. "You'll be fine. Give it a few weeks, and it'll all blow over. Has anyone told that Chardonnay woman, or whatever she's called?"

"No, not yet, I don't think."

"Well, you tell her. It'll make you feel better having a snipe at her, and you're still her boss, so she can't say anything."

I closed my eyes and sighed as the taxi pulled into my street. I was surprisingly sober. "No, I'm going to start the job hunt first thing."

"Oh, don't do that. You love your job."

I got out of the car and slammed the door. "I can't stay there knowing he could walk in any day. And what if Cara comes up to the office? God... I can't do it, Hayles."

She paid the fare, and I started digging in my bag for my keys as I walked up my drive. I tried not to look at the spot where my life was ruined, but I couldn't stop myself. "Why?"

She was at my side with her arm around my shoulders, nudging me away as I stared at the flagstone. "Nat…"

"Seriously, though. Why? What did I do to them to deserve this?"

She didn't reply. Instead she took my keys out of my hand and led me into the house.

I went straight up the stairs and stood in the doorway to my bedroom.

I'd let him in. I let him into my life, allowed myself to love him, and he'd done it to me again. Not in the same way, in many ways this was worse. The deceit. He'd hidden his entire life from me after coaxing the whole truth out of me. I should have known he couldn't be trusted after he failed to tell me about the company. Was I so lonely, so desperate to be loved, I was blind to the lies? I concluded I must have been. The disappointment in myself was far more destructive than my disappointment in him. And it was made infinitely worse by the fact that I missed him.

"Come on, you. Bed."

I did as she said, sitting cross-legged on the bed as she handed me a plate of toast.

She opened the window and looked out while I forced down some food. When I was done, I stuck the plate on the side. "What are you looking at?"

She turned and smiled at me. "Nothing. Get some sleep. I'll set your alarm so you get to work."

I groaned and lay back. "I'll have to walk in."

"Why? What did you do with your car?"

"I left it in the big car park."

She sucked in a breath. "That's gonna cost."

I turned on my side. I didn't care. Nothing mattered anymore. I couldn't remember feeling so empty. I was still fully dressed when she climbed into bed. I didn't care about that either. I was exhausted and I needed some sleep if I was going to survive the week.

## CHAPTER TWENTY-THREE

Tuesday was painful. Wednesday was slow. I drove home from work on Thursday ready to just sit down on the sofa and not move until Monday, but with one more day to go, I gave myself a pep talk. Get the week done, start the job search over the weekend. Something would turn up. It was just one more day, and it would all seem better on Monday.

All the motivation I'd built to finish the week died when I pulled into my drive to see a huge bunch of flowers sitting on my doorstep. The lump formed in my throat again and I steeled myself against the flood of emotions. I didn't know why I felt that way, I didn't even like flowers. He knew that. I distinctly remembered telling him. I supposed the feelings stemmed from knowing he was still trying to make me hear him out.

I got out of the car and approached the front door like it was dangerous. The flowers were pretty, probably cost a small fortune, and I noticed the little white envelope perched in the midst of the blooms as I picked up the arrangement. I slid the card from the envelope tucked inside. They were too little, too late. I didn't need them. I'd needed the truth, and while he was in a position to give me anything, it was the one thing he wasn't prepared to part with. I wasn't expecting a sonnet, but I was disappointed to see only three words written in softly looping handwriting, which I didn't recognize.

*I miss you*

Stuffing it among the blooms, I sniffed, and let myself in.

The house was silent. That used to bother me, but right then I was glad for it. I turned to place the flowers on the side table and almost dropped them when I saw the photograph lying on top.

I'd destroyed it. That image of Gav and I, standing in front of the old Rolls Royce we hired on our wedding day, smiling for the camera, shouldn't have existed

I stared at it, strangely numb to the fact that he'd been there. He wasn't supposed to be within miles of me, but he'd been inside my house. I should have been terrified. I should have been screaming and running from the building, but I knew that if I let the terror in, I'd never get it to go away. After a minute or so, I closed my eyes and took in a breath, forcing myself to stay calm, and then I put the flowers down beside the picture and went into the kitchen. Hanging my bag on the back of a dining chair, I set about pouring a glass of wine. It was probably a bad idea with all that was happening, I was safer keeping a clear head, but I needed to calm my jumping nerves.

Standing by the sink, I took three large gulps of wine and was interrupted by a message from Haylie. She'd spent Monday night with me, but I wouldn't let her stay Tuesday or Wednesday. I still hadn't heard the details about what had changed between her and Tommo, and certainly didn't want to rock the boat if they had everything back to normal, despite what was happening with my shitty life.

I moved back toward the living room and stopped in the doorway, staring at the flowers as I sipped my wine. My head was swimming, whether it was from the wine or stress, I couldn't quite tell.

I was so angry, not just at Jason for deceiving me, but also myself for allowing it to go that far. And at Gav for invading my life. He wasn't supposed to be within miles of me, yet he had the gall to come into my house. Bastard.

I'd been through enough, hadn't I?

Yeah, I was feeling sorry for myself. There wasn't anyone left to do it for me. My phone went off in the kitchen, but I ignored it. I knew it was Haylie checking in. Having my back in any way she could.

I went back to the sofa and curled around my glass. Then I laughed. It was loud in the silence of the otherwise empty house, and the sound startled me, but I couldn't stop it.

Of all the weeks for everything to fall apart with Jase, it had to be this one. Of all the days, it had to be last Sunday. I shouldn't have been surprised. That was how my life worked. I fell down, I got up, and something pushed me down again. It was how it had always been.

I needed more.

Thinking back over the events of the previous few months, I drained my glass and went back to the kitchen. Seeing my phone, I remembered something from Monday. I knew Haylie could clarify, so I grabbed my phone, dialed, and waited.

"Hello?"

"What were you looking at on Monday night?"

"What?"

"Monday night, you opened the window and looked out into the street for ages. Why?"

She was quiet for a moment. I waited. "There was someone walking their dog. It was straining by your gate, determined to get into the garden. The guy dragged it away, and I got into bed. Why?"

"What sort of dog?"

"I don't fucking know... What's wrong, you're scaring me."

"Nothing. Just something someone said... Never mind."

"It looked like a greyhound," she said suddenly. "Nat, are you okay?"

I forced a lighter tone and lied through my teeth. "I'm fine. Looks like Jason sent flowers. My house smells like a funeral parlor."

"Do you need me to come over?"

"No. No, I need an early night. We'll sort something soon though, okay?"

She didn't sound convinced, but let me end the call.

Taking a pen, I picked the card back up and took the photograph, and scribbled on the blank side before rooting in the kitchen drawer for tape. When I found it, I went to the door, secured the two of them to it, and locked myself inside the house.

Then I went to the kitchen, I poured myself another glass of wine and looked at my reflection in the window. Perfect. It was all just perfect. I tipped the glass toward the other me that was staring back, smiled, and said, "Happy Anniversary."

That was when the hysteria set in.

I couldn't do it. I couldn't live through it again. I didn't want to do it alone. I didn't want to lose everything again.

I picked up my phone before I could talk myself out of it.


Jason.

I'd fucked up spectacularly. Again.

There was no reason for her to trust me, so I wasn't surprised when she ignored every email, message, and phone call. When I called from Poppy's phone and heard the pain in her voice, I knew for certain that was it. I'd lost her.

It had been five days since she ran from me, and I'd never felt so miserable. I had no one to blame but myself. It was my own cowardice that had done it. Tony had warned me, he'd pressed and pressed for me to tell her, but I'd seen the look in her eyes when she saw the photograph of Poppy on his wall, and I couldn't handle Nat rejecting her. As much as I loved Nathalie, Poppy was everything. I was where I was because I couldn't bring myself to leave her. I couldn't walk away knowing what it was like growing up in a broken home.

I'd lived with Cara's hatred for years for Poppy. I'd taken every snide remark and never acted on it for her. I was happy to not be enough for my wife, if I could be for my daughter. She needed her parents. I stayed.

It was easier knowing it wasn't Cara's fault. Not in the beginning, at least. It clearly wasn't enough, but I'd done my best to support her. She'd suffered terribly when the baby arrived. The depression and anxiety were crippling. Nothing I said or did helped, so we found someone who could. Cara trusted her therapist, so when she suggested separate rooms, I went with it. When she suggested Cara take weekends to be by herself, I went with it. When Cara got drunk and told me I'd been the one who ruined her life, I accepted it. It wasn't until I had my own appointment with her therapist that I fully saw the whole picture, and by then it was far too late. I had to work, that was an unavoidable reality. When I wasn't at work, I did whatever was necessary to support my struggling wife, and that was an accepted fact. But our unavoidable lifestyle fanned the flames of her condition and destroyed our marriage. There was no way to repair it.

I was lamenting the unfairness of it all when my phone rang. I expected it to be Tony, so when I saw her name, I steeled myself as I answered.

"It's me, I... I'm sorry to bother you. I just needed to hear your voice."

I knew that tone. I knew what that small tremor in her voice meant and reached for my shirt. "What's happened?"

"Did I give you a key on Friday night?"

I didn't understand. I was at my bedroom door, tugging my shirt over my head when I paused and answered, "No. I couldn't lock the house because you left with the keys... I'm sorry, but you told me not to be there, so I made sure I wasn't like you asked. Why?"

Her voice lowered, she said, "He's been in the house."

I didn't need her to elaborate. I knew who *he* was. But he was under a court injunction. Her ex-husband wasn't supposed to be within miles of her.

"Are you alone?" I looked at my watch as I sped down the stairs and turned to the kitchen door. "Okay, keep the doors locked, leave the keys in, and close the blinds. I'm on my way, and I'll call when I get there."

She sniffed and took a shaky breath. "Okay. I'm sorry, Jason, I didn't know who else to... I didn't need..."

"It's okay, I'm leaving now. I'll be as quick as I can."

"Okay. Thank you, I..."

I didn't want to end the call, but I couldn't drive and keep her calm at the same time. "It's okay, I know. I'll be there soon."

Cara was sitting at the table on her laptop when I strode into the kitchen, tucking my phone into my pocket. "What are you doing?"

"I have to go out. Can you tell Pops I'll call her after school tomorrow?"

She turned in the chair and glared at me. "At this hour? I didn't get an alert from either team, what could possibly have you leaving at this time of night?"

My concern for Nathalie was turning to rage at *him* for daring to go near her. Cara wasn't helping. "I'm needed elsewhere, it's urgent. I'll be back on Sunday as usual."

She sighed and turned back to her laptop. "Not even hiding your transgressions now? That's wonderful."

Trying not to react, I ran my hands over my face. "Cara, I don't have the time or the energy for this. I think we can both agree that after eight years of you living apart from me in as many ways as possible, that the only transgression here is your treatment of me in my own home. Excuse me, my girlfriend needs me."

She looked like I'd slapped her. I'd never mentioned it. All the times she'd blamed me, all the times she'd told me that her suffering was my fault, not to mention the times she'd attacked me, not once had I spoken up in my own defense. I supposed she had a point. It had taken both of us, and while Poppy was created out of love, the toll motherhood had taken on Cara had been destructive. I played a part in that. We brought Poppy into the world together and it was that which had destroyed her.

I didn't wait for her to spit a reply, continuing through the kitchen to the utility hall, and into to the garage. I decided on the BMW. I knew Nathalie didn't really like the thing, and my tires were likely to be slashed again, but it would get me there much faster and time was everything. When she needed someone, she called me, and I had a small window of opportunity to prove I could be there for her. I wanted to be there. I checked the time and my phone rang again. The call connected through the car's Bluetooth as I backed out of the garage.

"I'm on my way, babe."

"You don't… I mean I shouldn't have. I'm sorry, Jason, you don't have to come all this way…"

"I'm coming, and I'm not leaving until I know you're safe."

"But I was… I mean…"

I took a breath and turned out of the drive, speeding through the small town outside of Huntingdon where Cara had decided we should settle in.

"I'm coming. I'll always come to you when you need me, Nat. If I don't have you I… I love you. So, sit tight, I'll be there in an hour or so."

She was silent. I kept driving, just relieved to have her on the line, knowing she was okay. That she was waiting and safe.

I knew how soft it sounded, but I had to reassure her. I needed her to know so she could stop doubting. Yeah, I was good at making the wrong choice, but I'd always be there if she needed me. I wouldn't make that mistake again.

"I'll keep coming back, Nathalie. It's you. It always was. You're all I need."

The line went dead. I wasn't sure if that was a good or bad sign, but I didn't call her back. I could get there faster if I didn't have to talk.

\* \* \*

The phone rang and rang, but I wouldn't get out of the car until she answered. I didn't want to knock on the door and startle her. Then the front door opened.

I didn't waste any time going to her. I saw the photo attached to the front door but ignored it, closing and locking it behind me as she walked into the living room.

I followed and looked immediately at the flowers on the side table. It was a big bouquet, probably cost a fortune, and was definitely the kind of thing you'd send if you wanted to impress. He just didn't know Nat. "I thought you hated flowers?"

"I do," she said, picking at her finger nails. "I thought at first maybe you could have left them. Then I came inside and saw…" Her eyes filled with tears, but she blinked them away and murmured, "He left one of our wedding photos. I thought maybe you'd dropped a key, but I wasn't thinking and—"

She was rambling, her anxiety building. I cut her off. "Why would I send flowers when I know you hate them?"

She was fiddling with her hair and eventually looked up, tucking a few strands behind her ears. "Forget the flowers. I owe you an apology."

I wasn't sure why she felt that was the right time to apologize, and I shook my head, but she carried on talking.

"I overreacted. I was out of order, and I'm sorry."

It was clear she wanted to talk about it. She'd clearly had a few glasses of wine, either to steady her nerves or to give her some courage, and I knew she wouldn't give up until she'd said what she needed, so I spoke, "I didn't mention Poppy because you made it clear kids weren't… Well, it sounded like you weren't keen, which is fine, I mean not everyone can be bothered, can they?"

I watched as she sat on the edge of the sofa and ran her hands through her hair. "I don't hate kids, Jase. I'm not a witch."

I didn't say anything, looking at the flowers again. She went on with her explanation.

"When I said what I said, I meant I walked away from my marriage without kids but with other baggage. I don't think kids are an issue. I don't think your daughter would cause a problem between us, I just meant that I don't have kids. It was a blessing really, but I wanted them. I just lost the option when…"

"Lost?"

I could see on her face that I wouldn't like where this was going.

"Yeah. The accident…" Her expression changed at that word.

I was pretty sure mine had too. It wasn't an accident, she was deliberately run over by her ex-husband, but I knew she didn't know what other word to use to address the event.

She looked down at the floor but continued, "The bleeding, they couldn't stop it. It was bad, and they had to... I don't have a uterus. I'm not equipped to have children." There was so much emotion in her voice I could tell she was struggling, and she paused. I watched her warring with herself over how to word it. In the end she glossed over, but I fully understood. "I came to terms with kids not being an option a long time ago. But that doesn't mean I can't be around them. Your daughter wasn't the issue. It was your deceit."

I didn't know what to say. I had to say something, but the gravity of what she'd just said had floored me. I walked over to the window, parted the blinds, and looked out, before turning back to her. "What do you need?"

She looked down at her hands. "Haylie said she'd stay, but I just..." She paused and took a deep breath. "I just wanted you."

She looked up at me then, her eyes filled with sadness and fear.

I wasn't sure what to do. I wanted to hold her, to tell her it was all going to be okay. But it wasn't. I'd hidden things from her. Important things. I'd hurt her for a second time after I promised not to. Her psychotic ex had broken into her home, invading the one safe place she had.

But despite all my fuck ups, I was the person she called. I wasn't sure how to handle it. Her eyes only showed a fraction of what she must have been feeling, and as much as I wanted to take that pain away, I didn't know how. Not without making promises I clearly couldn't keep. She deserved more.

She broke the silence that had fallen on the room by saying, "I'm sorry I reacted the way I did."

I clenched my fist but didn't move from the window. She was apologizing to me after all I'd done, and while I had things to say, I couldn't seem to say them.

"I should have asked you. I should have discussed it when you—"

I had to clear my throat to speak. "Nat, that was all my fault. I fucked up. I was trying to find a way to tell you, but the longer it went on the harder it got and… I'm sorry."

Wiping tears from her eyes, she explainedd, "Yeah, you lied to me, Jase, but I understand why, I think. I handled that really badly, and while the damage is done, I just want you to know I'm sorry."

"Why would the damage be done? Nat, I've been trying to talk to you all week. I wanted to… I messed up. I should have been honest. I shouldn't have raised my voice. I shouldn't have let you drive away so upset."

"We both… We're a mess, Jase. I don't know…" She took a breath. "I'm going to put the kettle on."

I let her walk away. She needed a minute to think and the last thing I wanted was for her to lose her nerve and stop talking. I needed to hear what she had to say. We both needed the truth to be laid out, however uncomfortable it made us.

I was standing where she left me, my hands in my pockets looking at the flowers, when she came back and handed me a mug of steaming coffee. She stood next to me and looked at them also.

"They're an anniversary gift, apparently."

I set my jaw, fighting not to say what was on my mind. I hadn't known the date, I hadn't even known it was close. When I looked at her, she smiled and put her mug on the window sill before she bent to pick up the bouquet. "He's been hanging around, I think. He must have been the one who slashed your tires. Haylie saw him outside here recently, but she didn't recognize him. The Land Rover at the strip mall… He'll get bored soon."

She hoped. She didn't say it, but that was what it came down to.

I watched as she went into the kitchen and unlocked the back door, taking the flowers and dumping them in the trash outside. I moved into the kitchen, leaning against the countertop by the sink to be close if something startled her while she was outside.

She locked the door behind her and took out the key before saying, "There. Where they should be."

It was a touchy subject, but I had to say it. "You should call the police. There's a restraining order, he's breaking the law."

She shook her head, the strands of hair behind her ears coming loose and falling over her face again. "No. He won't bother me. Really, it's not worth the mess of involving them."

I didn't argue. Instead I asked, "What did it say?"

"I miss you."

I laughed and shook my head, rubbing my bottom lip with my thumb.

She pulled in her brows and queried, "What?"

"Looks like there's a club."

She managed a small smile and said, "I missed you, too."

That was all I needed to hear. I knew she wouldn't say it, so I asked, "Can we just start again?"

She laughed, choking back tears. "Again?"

I shrugged. "Third time lucky?"

I couldn't stop myself from grinning when she replied, "I'd like that."

Taking a few tentative steps toward her, I studied her face. "I'm moving out. I'm walking away from Cara and that whole mess, and I'm starting again with you if you'll have me. I have a daughter, and she's important, but I can love you both. We can make it work, Nat."

She kept her head down, stepping toward me, and I took her into my arms. The tension left her body as she cried silently into my chest, and I stroked her hair as I held her. I knew I should say something, but I couldn't. I didn't want her to step away. I'd missed her. The feel of her body against mine, the scent of her, the sound of her voice. I didn't want to be without her again.

"Will you stay?"

I kissed the top of her head and moved her back so I could see her face. "I'm not going anywhere. At least until Sunday. After that we'll work something out."

She looked up at me and smiled. "Home for date night."

And there it was. Her acceptance.

I swore then that I could be everything she needed. All I had to do was love her. The rest we could work out together.

## ABOUT THE AUTHOR

Thank you so much for reading.

If you enjoyed this novel please consider leaving a review.

I'm always thrilled to chat with my readers and would be thrilled if you sought me out on social media.

You can find my Facebook page here, https://www.facebook.com/Shaebanksromance/

And can sign up for my newsletter where you will hear first hand about new releases here www.shaebanks.com

Printed in Poland
by Amazon Fulfillment
Poland Sp. z o.o., Wrocław